TONIGHT
THEY COME

NARU K. WILLIAMS II

MILTON & HUGO L.L.C.
4407 Park Ave., Suite 5
Union City, NJ 07087, USA

Website: *www. miltonandhugo.com*
Hotline: *1- 888-778-0033*
Email: *info@miltonandhugo.com*

Ordering Information:
Quantity sales. Special discounts are granted to corporations, associations, and other organizations. For more information on these discounts, please reach out to the publisher using the contact information provided above.

Library of Congress Control Number:		2024924408
ISBN-13:	979-8-89285-280-7	[Paperback Edition]
	979-8-89285-281-4	[Hardback Edition]
	979-8-89285-279-1	[Digital Edition]

Rev. date: 11/05/2024

"Kate Barrow." Detective Frank Drake exchanged a worried look with his partner, junior detective Julie Benz. "Yes, sir, we know of her."

"Good," Topher Madsen, chief of the Gateway City Police Department, said grimly. "I need you two to check on her."

"What has she done now?" *Keep it respectful, Frank.*

"Nothing at the moment. But we got a noise complaint involving her home. From a concerned neighbor, believe it or not."

Didn't know she had *"concerned neighbors" anymore.* Frank checked his watch and motioned for Benz to stop the squad car.

"Will we have backup on the scene?" he asked.

"Be a little much to scramble that for something like this, don't you think?"

"It's Kate Barrow, sir. We don't know how this could go."

"I hear you. If you need backup, call it *after* checking out her home."

"Yes, sir," Frank said as he felt his ulcers flaring up. *Let's hope we won't have to.* "Chief, given what she's done—"

"I'm not asking you to tuck her into bed, Drake," Madsen said in an irritated voice. "Just check out the complaint. You see anything amiss, you call for backup. You don't, file a report and get gone."

I know that look. Detective Benz's gray eyes fixed on Frank as he put his phone away. "So … what did Chief Madsen say about Kate Barrow?"

"We gotta check on her."

She blinked in surprise, her mouth slightly open. "Are you serious?"

"As a heart attack," he answered. "Let's get to her house."

Benz put on the sirens and hit the gas, sending their car rocketing down the street. She saw the scowl on Frank's face as he looked out his passenger-side window. *We were talking about football earlier.* "Frank?"

"Hmm?"

"Why are we going to Barrow's house? Just asking."

"Noise complaint, believe it or not."

"By who?"

"A concerned neighbor."

"Didn't know she had—"

"Concerned neighbors, I know," Frank said as he massaged his eyes. "But apparently she does, so we gotta check on her."

"Right," Benz muttered under her breath. "Like it's gonna be that easy." *Our shift was almost over.*

"I know, all right?!" Frank snapped. "Department's been on pins and needles since—"

"Barrow shot and killed Brian Solomon, a fifteen-year-old kid?"

And the agony begins, Frank thought, rolling his eyes with dread. "Get it out, now, Benz. We can't talk about this when we see Barrow."

"Love to," she said passionately. "Did you know she never spent one night in jail?"

"I'm aware," came the patient response. "I read about it in the papers."

"Right, you were on vacation. Lucky bastard."

"Hey, I was due for a break," Frank said defensively. "If I didn't use my vacation days, I would've lost 'em." *God, does that sound callous.* "I can't help that one of us lost their head while I was gone." *And did she just call me a bastard?*

"That's one way to describe what she did," Benz said, keeping her eyes on the street.

"I'm not a fan of her, either, but we have to support her."

"Why?"

"Because she's a cop, like us," Frank answered. *Even if we don't want to.* He felt bad for her. No matter what Barrow did from then on, she would be known as the cop that killed a kid. No one gets over that, not fully anyway.

And people like Benz sure as hell didn't help.

2

"I'm surprised you even kept up with Barrow's trial," Benz said, giving him an odd look.

"Didn't have a choice," Frank said, fidgeting uncomfortably in his seat. "It made national news. Everyone was dubbing it 'the Solomon shooting.'" *Like it needed a catchy title to stick in people's minds.* "All that did was make a bad situation worse."

"It's called being a watchdog, Frank," Benz said as they left downtown. "That's the news's job."

"What? Putting an honest cop through the ringer?"

"Putting a spotlight on despicable behavior," Benz stated sharply. "Making sure people don't forget. You know, like we always do?"

"You mean, keeping people from moving on," Frank said sourly. "Thanks to those 'watchdogs,' Gateway City almost had a riot on its hands."

"Barrow's shooting is the seventh one by our department this year. I'd gladly take a riot if it kept shit like this from happening all the time."

"Am I gonna have to worry about you?"

Benz shot Frank a glance. "There a reason you should?"

"You're gripping the stirring wheel a little tight there, lady."

Her jaw clenched, curse words threatening to spill like water from a broken dam. *Use a light touch.* "Why? Because I know killing a kid's wrong on all fronts?" Her eyes were like daggers, daring him to disagree.

"I'm not contesting that," Frank said. "I'm just asking you to be professional."

"If Barrow had been professional, we wouldn't be doing this at all."

"Point proven," Frank admitted, shrugging his shoulders.

"Brian Solomon was innocent," Benz continued. "He was an innocent kid, and he was shot dead. On his property. Before his parents' eyes. And yet at Barrow's trial, people were treating them like they were the bad guys!"

"I know, Benz."

"Brian's father had to make an impassioned speech just to be treated fairly. Meanwhile, Mrs. Killer McGee sat with her lawyers, looking smug as a bug in a rug! And she was acquitted! Fucking acquitted! Is that really the system of justice we serve?!"

"You've only been a detective for a few months," Frank said, giving Benz a sympathetic look. "Give it a couple of years. You'll see how things really are."

"And what am I gonna see?" Benz asked, keeping her gaze focused on the road. She couldn't afford to look at Frank when she was angry, not if she wanted his respect. He was a damn good detective, and a better mentor.

He showed her how to handle paperwork, how to talk to victims, and how to interrogate suspects properly. But they differed so much on their view of the badge.

Frank believed it was an honor, and ironclad. He also believed in cops supporting one another. Someone was either blue, or they weren't.

And if they weren't blue, they needed to shut up about things they didn't understand. And be grateful while doing it.

Benz, on the other hand, believed that wearing a badge made you part of the law, not above it. And it didn't give anyone an excuse to do what they wanted and hide from the consequences.

That's what Kate Barrow had done.

And the GCPD was suffering the consequences.

"We'll be at Barrow's house `in a little bit," Frank declared, noticing they had passed a familiar street sign. "This out of your system? Or will you need to stay in the car when I talk to her?"

Benz sighed and looked at Frank with finely concealed disgust. "How long did it take you?"

"To what?"

Don't you say it, Frank thought, knowing what was coming with that holier-than-thou look in her eyes. *Don't you freaking say it.*

"To get so whipped by the job?"

She freaking said it! "Watch it, Benz," Frank snapped, fire in his eyes. *I'm the freaking senior detective, and she disrespects me like this!*

"I'm just saying," he continued in a calmer voice, "seeing complex situations in black-and-white terms is what causes problems."

"Shooting an innocent kid and getting off for—it isn't complex," Benz muttered as she turned into Kate Barrow's neighborhood. "It's just plain wrong."

"And what if you were in her shoes?" Frank asked, shooting her an accusing look. "What if you found yourself on trial for an accidental shooting?"

"An accidental shooting," she said, shaking her head in disbelief. "You should listen to how you sound, right now."

It was, though! Frank thought defensively. "Answer the question, Benz."

"I'd pray to God I'd be punished accordingly. Anything less is just an excuse."

"How'd I know you'd say that?" Frank asked exasperatedly.

"What would you do if Barrow killed one of your kids?"

Benz's question gave Frank pause. It was one he had been asking himself as he read about Kate Barrows' trial.

What would he do if he were in the position of Stan and Francine Solomon, the parents of the child whom Barrow had killed? What if he was the one begging the jury to put Barrow away as Stan had done while his wife looked like a haunted wreck?

That fact that Stan had to convince the jury to see his side when he was the victim—was that really justice?

It was one thing to tout some company-sponsored response, but Benz knew Frank better. She knew he would give the question real thought and give an actual answer.

From his gut.

"Well, Benz, to tell you the—"

"Hold up," she said, interrupting him. "We're here."

You did not just cut me off! Frank looked out the window, recognizing the identical houses of the cul-de-sac called the Grove. "Yep, we are."

"Kate Barrow lives here?"

"Uh-huh."

"What kind of investments does she possibly make to be able to afford this place?!" Benz exclaimed. "The houses look like two-story palaces!"

"Jeez, enough!" Frank snapped. "Some people know how to spend their money wisely! Now, can we drop this so we can check on one of our own?!"

Benz looked ready to pounce on him but instead turned her gaze straight ahead.

Dammit. Frank sighed through acidic pangs of guilt. It was bad enough Kate Barrow's bullshit was taking his time, he didn't need Benz making him feel worse.

But that didn't give him cause to snap at her. He was the senior detective. He had to show a better example. "Look, Benz—"

"Frank," she asked, her voice heavy with apprehension. "Where'd this come from?"

—⚋—

Where'd this storm come from? Benz wondered as she stared out their windshield.

Gateway City, normally a sunny place, had been overcast for the past week. The skies were a light ash gray, a color that looked out of place to her eyes.

It put her on edge.

And worse? There'd been no rain. Not even a light fog.

Weather forecasters were clueless, and everyone else was getting nervous.

Crime had increased because of it, as if people were venting pent-up frustrations. Benz and Frank had just come from a domestic dispute when Madsen called. Benz glanced at the cut on her arm where an angry wife had slashed at her while trying to stab her husband.

Why? Because she thought he was having an affair.

He thought she was an uppity bitch, called her that to her face.

A surefire way to put anyone on the warpath.

It got so intense that Benz and Frank had to call for backup, putting both spouses in the wagon for processing back at the station.

And then they saw the kid, cowering under the dinner table, waiting for his parents to stop fighting.

This is Kate's fault, Benz remembered thinking as she coaxed the young boy out from his hiding place. *Her verdict's making everyone think they can get away with murder.*

And yet, that wasn't entirely it.

For a reason she couldn't explain, Benz knew—just knew—the sky was the real culprit. That it had somehow given the couple the nudge they needed to attack one another in front of their child.

The idea of it shook her so bad that she and Frank had to joke about football to relieve the tension.

What Benz saw over Kate Barrow's house brought the idea back, in full force.

—⁂—

"What the ..." Frank saw, to his surprise, that they were heading into a raging storm. He looked behind them, saw relatively dry skies. He looked ahead, saw angry storm clouds. "What the hell?"

"No kidding," Benz agreed as she slowed the car a little.

We might wanna turn ..., Frank thought before a bright flash made him jump. *Holy shit!*

Then came another flash ...

And another ...

And another ...

And another!

Happens all the time, Frank thought, looking for assurance that Kate's noise complaint would be like any other he had handled. *Nothing out of the ordinary, here ...*

Then he saw the lightning bolts strike the area around Barrow's house.

In a freaking circle!

"I'm no meteorologist ..." Benz started as she stared at something she had no doubt been convinced couldn't happen.

"But lightning doesn't do that," Frank finished. "I'm thinking the same thing." Did he see the beginnings of a funnel cloud over Barrow's roof?

"I know I'm new to Gateway City," Benz whispered, "but *is* this normal?"

Frank shot her a look of disbelief. "Are you seriously joking, right now?"

"Trying to relieve tension," she answered, her eyes on the turbulent skies. "Because I'm a breath step away from turning this car around and flooring it out of here."

"I get it," Frank said, his eyes back on Barrow's home. "But I'm not about to let a light show keep me from doing my job."

"I am," Benz said as she cautiously eased their squad car forward.

They stopped the car in front of Kate's home, rain pelting the windshield. Benz gave the front door a pensive look. "I still think we should call for backup."

"For what? A little rain?"

"Did you not *see* the lightning?"

"We don't know if it's connected with Kate."

"It's over her house!" Benz declared emphatically. "And nowhere else!" Her eyes were wide with disbelief, her mouth agape as she looked from Barrow's home to Frank. *I know you're dedicated to the job, but come on!*

"Coincidence," Frank stated, refusing to meet her eyes. "You'll see worse. For now, focus on the job in front of us."

"Right," Benz said, resigned to their course of action. She glanced behind her and saw …

No one.

The streets behind them were dearth of people.

Usually a police presence gets some attention! The human animal liked to watch, to observe. It was coded, right down to the DNA.

So where was everyone?

This is wrong, Benz thought, her apprehension increasing. *We shouldn't be here.* She felt as though they were about to pass through the veil. As though they were about to leave the land of reason and common sense and head into a world of madness and worse.

And she had no idea why.

Call it women's intuition.

—◊◊—

"Once again, how can she afford this?" Benz asked quietly. "She's a beat cop, for crying out loud!"

Kate Barrow's home was a two-bedroom house on a dead-end street, with the rest of the houses on its right and left. It was big, the kind that Frank saw in the sitcoms he watched when he was a kid. It had gables, dormers, a screened-in front porch, a free-standing garage, and even a garden.

The ultimate expression of the American dream.

"Rich parents help," he answered. "And don't underestimate how much beat cops get paid. It would blow your mind."

"Care to try again?"

"There's a college, a few blocks from here," Frank admitted finally. "Sometimes Kate rents out the extra bedrooms for extra cash."

"She has extra bedrooms?"

"Yup."

"Gotta give it to her," Benz said. "She's got good business sense."

"No kidding. Now can we please focus?"

"Right, sorry," she said. "What's the plan?"

"We do a perimeter sweep," Frank answered. "You take right, I'll take left. We meet in the front of the house and compare notes. Be on the lookout for anything funny."

"Thought you said this would be simple."

"It will be," he insisted as he got out of the car. "But no sense being complacent."

"I hear that," she said, following his lead.

Frank shivered as the rain soaked their suit-and-tie clothes. The only protection they had were their trench coats, his being a dark brown while, Benz's was a light tan. They also wore rain slickers, but all they did was make them smell like waterlogged tires.

"Shouldn't we just knock on Barrow's door?"

We should, Frank agreed, *but ...* "We're doing the sweep first."

"Any reason why?"

"Peace of mind."

Maybe it was the rain. Or the lightning. Or the cloak-and-dagger way Madsen gave them the assignment. Whatever it was, Frank felt it was better to be safe than sorry.

—⚏—

Benz took the left side of the house, feeling pretty stupid. *We're just prolonging this! Let's just knock on her door, for God's sake!*

The grass around Kate's home was thick. And the rain made the ground muddy, making her feel as though she was stepping into quicksand. A few times, she damn near slipped. *Swear to God if I break something ...*

"Benz," Frank called out from her shoulder communicator.

"Yeah?"

"Didn't Barrow have a guard detail here? To keep out the protesters?"

"I believe so."

"You see *any* hint of them?"

"I haven't finished my side yet," Benz answered grimly. "But no. You?"

"Not even used cigarette butts," Frank answered.

"Cigarette butts?"

"You don't have guards to your home without a few of them needing a smoke break. And given how eager Kate is to please people, she would've let them smoke."

"She's becoming more likable by the minute," Benz grumbled under her breath. *Why are we going to all this trouble for this woman? And why'd Madsen request our help when he knew our shift was ending? There are other detectives he could've called! Patrol officers could've done this! Hell, patrol officers should be doing this, not seasoned detectives!*

The whole thing rubbed Benz the wrong way. It felt as though she and Frank were doing something that Madsen didn't want the rest of the department to know about.

"You hear that?" Frank asked, cutting through her thoughts.

"Can barely hear anything over this freaking rain."

"I mean from inside the house."

Benz put her ear close to a nearby window. "No."

"Exactly," Frank agreed. "We're here because of a noise complaint..."

"And yet the interior of the house is silent," Benz finished. *That can't be good.*

"Meet me back at the front."

"On my way."

—∞—

"How do you want to do this?" Benz asked a few minutes later as she and Frank stood outside Kate Barrow's front door.

"Knock," he answered. "Kate should respond. We make sure she's all right, maybe issue a warning. Then we radio Madsen and get out of here."

"Madsen specifically?"

"He's taking a hands-on approach to this," Frank said, shrugging his shoulders. *Now that I think of it, that is pretty suspicious. Something to look into later.*

"Mrs. Barrow," Benz called out, knocking firmly on the door. "We got a noise complaint from one of your"—her voice trailed off as the front door quietly swung open—"neighbors."

Seeing that made Frank whip out his sidearm.

Benz did the same, eyeing him for instruction.

Step inside, he mouthed quietly. "Carefully." Frank waited with bated breath, 9mm ready as Benz stepped through the door.

Then he released his breath when she didn't step out.

"Benz?" Frank whispered into his communicator.

No answer.

"Benz!" He was about to run back to the car when a pair of hands grabbed him and yanked him through the door.

—∞—

"Ummph!" Frank grunted as he found himself thrown against a wall.

11

A kick to the midsection doubled him over. It was followed by a haymaker across his face that sent him flying across the room. *Shit!* The same hands lifted Frank up, only to dash him against the floor, his 9mm flying from his hand. *Too fast!*

"Honey," a female voice said. "Let's show some restraint, huh?"

"I will when they do, honey," a baritone voice answered.

To Frank's gratitude, the attack ceased, giving him a chance to breathe. He found himself on the floor, sprawled in what looked like Kate's living room. He saw a television to his right and a sofa at his feet, flanked by two easy chairs. He tried to get up, but pain from his injuries made it a challenge.

"I'd stay down if I were you, friend," the baritone voice warned.

Yeah, think I'll do that, Frank thought, looking up at his attacker.

Standing over him was a large African American man dressed like those superheroes from the movies. He even had a cape that draped down his back and ended at his feet.

You're Stan Solomon, Frank realized, the color draining from his face. *Father of the kid Kate killed. Which means …* He looked to the man's left and saw a red-haired woman with striking blue eyes standing next to him. *You're Francine Solomon.* He saw Benz in the corner. REALLY *wish we'd called for backup!*

—⟋⟍—

We should've radioed for backup, Benz thought groggily as she found herself across from Frank in Kate's living room. She was on the floor, same as him. The difference was that she was in restraints while he was free.

If one counted gasping for breath while looking up at two pissed-off parents as free.

It had happened so fast. One second she had stepped into a darkened house, just in time to notice four pinpricks of light to her left …

The next, Benz was on the floor, metal pipes wrapped around her arms and legs. *How'd they do this so fast?*

They must have knocked her out; it was the only way they had been able to restrain her without a fight. They must have been fast too—they had pulled Frank into the house a few seconds after her.

No, not them. Stan and Francine Solomon.

They looked a hell of a lot different from how the papers had described them.

They had said Stan was tall, but that didn't do him justice. Stan Solomon was big. The dark suit he wore revealed muscles he didn't have at Barrow's trial. It looked to be made of sculpted spandex, giving him a superheroic look under the lights of Barrow's home.

Benz's eyes fastened onto the symbol on his massive chest, looking like an upside-down triangle. Inside was a bird with outstretched wings, whose tips touched the corners.

Francine was dressed like her husband. She even sported the same chest symbol, except her triangle was right side up. That, and it was slightly stretched, thanks to her cleavage.

That, Benz had to admit, had gotten her attention first.

For a minute, she wasn't sure either of the Solomons could have attacked her. They looked too ornate for assault.

Then her eyes caught the minute arcs of electricity snaking across their bodies. It was the same color as the lightning outside Kate's home.

What had Chief Madsen gotten her and Frank into?

—⟶⟶—

Someone's taken their love of superhero movies too far. "Benz?" Frank called out. "You okay over there?"

"Fine," came the sarcastic reply. "Just freaking gumdrops and ice cream over here."

Can always count on your coping skills, Frank thought as he looked to Stan and Francine. *Wait a minute, are they glowing?!* He shut his eyes tight, then opened them again. *Yup, they're glowing! How the hell are they glowing?!*

"Their backup will be here soon," Stan said.

"You don't know that," Francine said.

13

"They were sent here by Madsen. They don't report in, he'll send more."

"Right," Francine answered wearily. "Good point."

They're on a first-name basis with our chief, Frank thought. *Not a good sign.*

"Stan and Francine Solomon? You're both under arrest."

Stan shot him a look, and Benz and chuckled.

"Good one, Detective."

He thinks I'm joking. "I'm serious, asshole."

"And I'm still laughing, you son of a bitch."

"Where's Kate?" Frank demanded. "We know you're here for her."

Stan and Francine exchanged irritated looks.

"Told you we should've left the minute we had her," he said.

"I know, I know," Francine said, rolling her eyes.

"Where is she?!" Frank called out.

"Be quiet," Stan snapped, turning his back to him.

Francine gave the detective a sour look. *Oh no, he did NOT just turn his back on me!* "I'm talking to you!" Frank tried to get up, but knives of pain forced him back to the floor. *Dammit! What'd he do to me?!* "Please," Benz spoke up from where she was. "Can you tell us if she's all right?"

Don't beg them, Benz! Frank thought, only for Francine to point to the couch in the middle of the room.

"She's right here."

—ᴧᴧ—

Kate Barrow, a person that hurt the GCPD worse than any internal affairs probe, sat unconscious on the couch in front of the Solomons. Her head leaned to one side, and her body was bound by bent metal pipes.

We must've gotten here right after they wrapped her up, Benz thought. *And they did NOT spare the rod.*

An ugly bruise hung just above Kate's left eye, making her head look lopsided. Her arms were covered in cuts and bruises while her pajamas were caked in patches of dirt, soot, and grime.

She must've fought them. The Solomons hit like a hammer, and she fought them. The noise tipped off the neighbors. One of them called Madsen, and he called us. Benz took a quick glance around the living room, trying to connect Kate's injuries with any damages she saw.

The woman-sized indentations in the walls implied that Stan and Francine tossed her around a few times before tying her up. Given how strong Stan showed himself to be when he roughed Frank up, it wasn't hard to see why Kate was unconscious.

A clap of thunder pulled Benz out of her inspection. She saw raindrops outside, pelting Kate's apartment like stones.

We're trapped, she realized. *In here, with the Solomons. And we're unarmed. At least not with any weapons that could do them damage.*

Benz shot Frank a glance, noting the pained wheezing coming from his lips. *And he's really hurt.* She winced as she tried to move while still lying on her side in the corner of the room.

Right where the Solomons had left her.

"Mr. and Mrs. Solomon," Benz said in a soft voice. "You have to stop this."

"Fat chance," Stan said over his shoulder.

"I'm sorry about Brian. I really am."

Francine turned to her. "That's … very kind of you to say," she said, her voice revealing an inner warmth.

"More than most," Stan agreed, his expression callous.

Keep going! "And Kate's sorry too. I know she is."

"Sorry's not the same as punished."

"She should've gone to jail for what she did," Francine stated, her voice thick with emotion. "But she didn't. Not for a single night."

"And I know that's tearing her up inside,' Benz said sympathetically. *Least it better be.*

"She didn't care," Stan spat. "None of you do. Her show trial proved that."

"We absolutely *do* care. We'd do anything to fix what happened."

"Can you bring our son back, Detective?" Francine asked pointedly. "Can you raise him from the dead?"

—※—

15

Superhumans. Frank's brain was having a hard time wrapping itself around the idea. *I'm looking at two honest-to-God superhumans!*

He would read about them in comic books. He never thought he would see them in real life. *And of course, they're crazy.* He gritted his teeth as a sharp pain hit his side. *How'd they even get powers, anyway? How can anyone get powers like that? And how long have they had them?*

They couldn't have had them before their son was killed. They would have to have gotten them after. But who gave them these powers?!

One way to find out. "So how'd you get your powers?"

"Excuse me?" Stan asked, fixing Frank an evil look from the middle of the room.

Jesus Christ, his eyes are glowing! "I said, how'd you get your powers?"

"What makes you think I'd tell you?"

"Idle conversation?"

Stan scowled. "Are you testing me?"

There were so many ways Frank could've answered that, and none of them would've been in his best interest. Usually, on a case, all he had to do was provoke a suspect, keep him angry and off balance while Benz came in for the win. It was the dynamic they had established early in their partnership, and it always led to closed cases.

But that had to be thrown out the window, especially with Stan's strength and mad-on for Gateway City's finest. Provoking Stan would make a dicey situation worse.

But if Frank couldn't provoke him, what could he do? *I gotta confront him. With extreme caution. I can't take any more hits from this guy.*

"Well?"

"Humor me. I'm curious."

"Friend ..." Stan moved from Francine's side in the middle of the room to Frank near the exit, in the time it took the detective to blink. "You don't get to be curious."

He yanked Frank off the floor by his shirt collar and pinned him against the wall. "We're way past that."

—∿—

Nice, Frank, Benz thought. *Real sensitive*. She struggled against her bonds while lying on her side. *These bent pipes still aren't giving an inch.*

Fleeing and fighting was out, if Stan's little display of power was any indication.

That left talking.

But would either of the Solomons listen?

"What Kate Barrow did to your child was terrible," Benz started. *Please listen!* "But it was an error in judgment—that's all it was!"

"That left our son *dead*," Francine declared. "You keep glossing over *that* part."

"Killing Barrow's not going to make you feel better. And it won't bring Brian back."

"Neither will ignoring his death," Stan shot back. "Or the one that killed him."

"Besides," Francine added. "what makes you think we're going to kill her?"

So this is a kidnapping. "You've got superstrength, speed, and who knows what else," Benz reasoned. "If you really wanted to take Barrow, you would've done it already."

"We were about to," Stan admitted. "but my wife wanted to 'talk' to her."

"I wanted to know why she killed our son," Francine admitted. "She's a police officer. She's supposed to protect him, and she killed him. I wanted to know why."

"Baby, no matter what she tells us, it won't be enough."

"It'll never be enough," Benz cut in. She knew that like any couple going through grief, Stan and Francine had gone through this conversation before. Many times, in fact. So much, in fact, that having the conversation again wouldn't bring the Solomons any new insight.

Not when they had the target of their anger gift-wrapped in front of them.

But if Benz could keep the conversation going, the Solomons wouldn't leave. Not until it was finished. And that would give Madsen time to bring help.

Besides, the Solomons *needed* to talk. To explain themselves to anyone that would listen. Benz knew she couldn't get through to them. But if she got them into custody, she could find someone who could.

"Nothing could ever be enough," she continued, her voice a mixture of explanation and plea. "Including kidnapping Kate. And where would you take her, anyway? There's nowhere on Earth you could take her that we, or any other law enforcement agency, wouldn't find her."

"That's why we're taking her *off* Earth," Francine revealed.

—⚏—

Jesus. Frank gawked at Stan. *Can they … do that?*

Stan turned to him and nodded, as if he had heard Frank's thoughts.

Wait, *did* Stan hear Frank's thoughts?! Could they do that too?! *Oh, this can't happen!*

"Stan," Frank said in an urgent voice, "you have to stop this."

"Did I say you could call me by my first name?"

Asshole! "Fine! Mr. Solomon! I get your son's death was terrible, but think about what you're unleashing here!"

"What would you know about unleashing anything?" Stan asked, but it looked as though he was listening.

"You served in the war in Iraq!" Frank hissed, his face a mask of growing desperation. "You know what it's like to make a bad call! I'm sure you've made more than your fair share! We all have!"

"And?"

"Do you really want to punish Barrow for doing something you and me have done ourselves?"

A troubled look danced across Stan's dark features.

"You think this will make Gateway City better?! Every two-bit nutjob with a grudge will come out of the woodwork, inspired by you two! It'll be chaos!"

"You don't know that."

"Gateway City nearly cracked open after Barrow's acquittal!" Frank said. "Imagine what will happen if you *kidnap* her! The city will self-destruct!"

"Or maybe people will learn there are consequences for bad behavior," Stan said in a no-nonsense, stern voice. "No matter their skin color, background …"

"Dammit, Stan!"

"Or how rich their family is."

Frank blinked as if he had been slapped. "Huh?"

"Don't act ignorant. I know Barrow's from a rich family," Stan snapped. "One that has a lot of pull in this town. And they used that influence to get her off for killing our son. If such a thing can happen, maybe it's time for Gateway City to experience a little more chaos. Least my wife and I won't be suffering alone."

—⦿—

"Think of your family," Benz pleaded, giving Francine the best puppy-dog eyes she could muster.

"I think of nothing but," Francine insisted, giving her a wary glance.

"I meant your *surviving* family! You'll be putting a target on them if you do this!"

Francine gave Benz a skeptical look before breaking into laughter.

Not the reaction I wanted, Benz thought apprehensively. *Why is she laughing?!*

"Thanks, Detective," Francine said when she finished. "It feels so good to laugh."

"I'm serious," Benz insisted. "Think about your families! Both of them!"

"My 'family' hasn't spoken to me since I married Stan. Because he's black, in case you're wondering."

No, I put that together myself, Benz thought, giving her a sympathetic look. "Whatever they think of your union with Stan, they can't deserve the firestorm that'll come if you abduct a police officer from her home!"

"The only family I care about is Stan's," Francine declared, titling her head at her husband. "And they've endured much worse than simple public backlash."

"Backlash is never simple, Mrs. Solomon." *Trust me on that.*

19

—⦚—

C'mon, Chief, don't let us down! Frank glanced out of a nearby window, seeing lightning bolts continuing to strike the ground outside of Barrow's house.

Were they getting closer?

Why are there no bystanders?

Someone called in the first noise complaint to get him and Benz to the scene. Had no one called in a second one?!

"I wouldn't overthink it," Stan suggested. "It's beyond you."

"Okay, *how* are you doing that?" Frank demanded. "Are you reading my mind?"

"No. I just know body cues when I see them."

Yeah, right, Frank thought. *How am I supposed to arrest someone that knows what I'm gonna do before I do?*

—⦚—

"You know what *is* simple?" Francine asked. "Good, old-fashioned racism."

I wondered when she would pull on that branch, Benz thought, her brow furrowing in anger. *It always seems to come back to that.*

"That woman killed my son," Francine continued, glaring at Kate behind her. "And got away with it. And you know why? Because she's a white cop and Brian was a black boy."

"I can see why you'd believe that." *I was just talking to Frank about that, earlier.*

"Are you contesting me?"

"Not even a little," Benz answered, hoping her sympathy came off genuine.

"I didn't believe it at first," Francine continued. "I mean, it's 2023! We're supposed to be past all that!"

"That's for damn sure."

"I mean, I knew racism existed, I'm not an idiot, but I never knew it was so …" She took a moment to let out an angry whimper. "Ingrained."

I guess we never really outgrow our old habits, Benz thought sadly. *We just convince ourselves that we do.*

"But Brian's death? It made me realize something," Francine went on. "Nobody wants to confront racism. To do anything about it. They just want to say they do."

Time to reign her in. "That's not true, Mrs. Solomon."

"I was like them once, I was! I never thought racism would ever touch us! Stan was in the military! I was a teacher! We were law-abiding citizens! Surely the law would be on our side no matter what! That's how it's supposed to work!"

She's not even listening to me, Benz realized, closing her eyes regretfully. *She's talking just to vent.*

"I dismissed the shootings on the news," Francine continued in a rant. "Other people of color have been killed by police. But I never thought that would happen to us. Because those people? Surely they did something to deserve it, right?! But we'd *never* put ourselves in such a terrible situation!"

"You're not the only one who's thought that," Benz agreed, her eyes full of sympathy, "only to be proven wrong."

"I had *so* much faith in the law," Francine finished, laughing through the last of her words.

And she's gone. "It's not a perfect system, but—"

"Then I lost Brian. My Brian! In such a *senseless* way!" Francine turned from Benz to Kate, her eyes as cold as an executioner's. "And I'm not so faithful anymore."

—◆—

"Don't lose faith in the law," Kate Barrow whispered, waking up at last. "It's … all we have."

No! Frank thought, his eyes wide with alarm. *Not now!*

Everyone cocked their heads toward Kate as she spoke, sounding younger than her twenty-nine years. "Let them go. It's me you—"

"Shut up," Francine said as she clamped a hand around Kate's throat. "Shut up! Shut up! Shut the *hell* up!"

"I went to Brian's gra—ahhhhh!" Kate let out a banshee wail as arcs of electricity struck her body from Francine's fingers. The malicious current crawled across the floor, walls, and ceiling of the living room.

Some even hit Stan's legs, but he didn't seem to mind.

"Goddammit, Stan, stop her!" Frank begged. "She's gonna kill her!"

"You don't *get* to feel guilty!" Francine roared as tears ran sizzling down her cheeks. "You didn't care about him! You didn't raise him! You didn't *know* him!"

"I know why you wear—ahhhhh!" Kate got out before another surge of electricity hit her.

"Shut the hell up! You don't *get* to apologize! It won't save you!"

"Tell her to stop!" Frank whispered frantically to Stan. "Please! Just tell her to stop!"

"Dammit," Stan muttered under his breath. "Francine! Enough! We need her alive!"

"Why?!" she thundered, shaking the living room. "Why does she get to live when Brian didn't?!"

"We kill her like this, and we're no better than she is," Stan thundered back, stomping his foot. "Is that what Brian would want?"

"I …" Francine blinked, her grip wavering.

"Is this what he would want?!"

"I …" She swallowed awkwardly. "No." She let go of Kate, stepping away from her as if she was poison. "No, he wouldn't."

"Good, baby." Stan let Frank drop from his grip as though she was a sack of dirty clothes to the floor as he went to comfort Francine. "Good."

"I hate her," Francine declared, melting into him as though he was a life preserver. "I hate her so much!"

"I know, baby," Stan cooed quietly, stroking her hair. "I know."

Jesus Christ! Frank thought as he stared at Kate Barrow. "Barrow! Are you all right? Talk to me!"

Kate was smoking, lost to a coughing fit as she tried to breathe. Finger-shaped burns encircled her neck in a collar of raw skin. It was a damn miracle her pajamas hadn't burst into flames from Francine's electricity.

—⟋⟍—

We can't win this, Benz realized, feeling sick. *Not our own. Stan and Francine are way too powerful. And too angry.* That Francine tortured Kate so readily showed she was too far gone for talking.

She and Stan both.

Yeah, we're not gonna win this. Benz struggled against her bonds. She shot Frank a no-nonsense look. *Unless one of us loses.*

—◆◆◆—

Benz, are you asking me to … Frank looked to the door, which was still open. *She can't be …* Escape was so close. *How am I supposed to even …*

Then he remembered he wasn't tied down, not like Benz and Kate were.

Wait a second, why wasn't he tied down?

Frank tentatively tried moving his leg, only for white-hot pain to crawl up his body like a swarm of angry ants. *Right! That's why!* Stan had beaten him bad enough that moving was going to be a problem. *I guess the missus is getting too volatile for him to worry about little old me.*

—◆◆◆—

Just run, Benz thought, giving him an impatient look. She glanced at the Solomons, then back at Frank. *Just fucking run!*

—◆◆◆—

"What were you thinking?" Stan asked as he rocked Francine in his arms. "You wanted to talk to her, remember?"

"I know," she said, shaking her head. "I just wanted to make sense of it. Thought she could help me do it." She clenched her jaw. "It was stupid, I know. The detective was right. It won't bring Brian back. I don't know what I was thinking."

"You were doing what you always do," Stan answered as he looked into her eyes. "You look for light in the darkest moments. Justice in the most … unjust of circumstances." He brushed the hair out of her eyes, a gentle smile on his face. "It's why I love you." He looked dispassionately

23

at Barrow. "But there's no light here. The only justice we can count on is our own."

"That's a sorry commentary in itself."

"I know. Welcome to my world."

—ɷ—

They're only gonna be distracted a little while longer, Benz thought, gesturing to the apartment's exit with her head. *Get out of here now and get help!*

I'm not leaving you behind, Frank thought, his eyes following Benz's gaze. *There has to be another way!* And yet he saw none. If the Solomons were willing to torture a cop on a whim, there was nothing they wouldn't be willing to do.

And the power at their command? Nothing he or Benz had in their arsenal could combat that.

Retreat was the best option.

But Frank would be damned if he left Benz to the Solomons! What if they took her and Kate when he was gone? What if his leaving pushes them to do something worse? *Dammit, why aren't the reinforcements here?!*

Why did Madsen drop this case in their hands? Why did he put Benz and Frank in this terrible situation? This wasn't a case for detectives, no matter how seasoned! This was a case for the marines! The army!

Hell, an exorcist! A team of them!

—ɷ—

"Stan, if what she said was true …" Francine said, a look of doubt playing across her face. "If what we do comes back on our family …"

"You want to stop, we can," Stan declared, standing with her in the middle of the living room. "You put us on this path, you can take us off it. But we can't return these powers."

"They're ours for life, I know."

"So?"

"We stay the course," Francine decided after a few moments of thought. "Not just for Brian, but for all the people of Gateway City."

She squared her shoulders, as if preparing for battle. "We can help them with these powers. It's what Brian would want."

"Then we *will* help them," Stan said, furrowing his brow with deadly purpose. "We'll make sure what happened to Brian won't happen to anyone else ever again."

—⋙—

That's all I need to hear. There was no time for Frank to get his gun. All he had time to do was run. Get to his feet, run for the exit for all he was worth, and get to their car.

He would call for backup on the radio.

Give me a distraction. He nodded to Benz. *And make it Oscar-worthy. Here we go.*

"There are better ways to help people than this!"

Stan and Francine turned to face Benz, perhaps eager to hear what she had to say. She had them on a string. Shame she had to use it to trick them.

—⋙—

Frank went for the door, pushing his injured body as far as it could go.

"Looks like we got a runner," Stan declared, turning to watch him run.

A bolt of heat caught Frank in the shoulder, sending him flying out of the apartment and into the wind and rain. He hit Barrow's front yard hard, bolts of pain shooting through his shoulder. *Damn!* Blinking stars from his vision, he looked through a wall of water …

To see a police blockade in front of Barrow's house, fog lights on the windows.

"They got … hostages," he wheezed as two officers ran to get him away from the line of fire. "One's Benz …"

"It's okay," the closest one said, grabbing one shoulder while his partner grabbed the other. "We got you."

"And Kate. Gotta … save 'em …"

"We know, man. Madsen scrambled us when you didn't report in."

What took you so long? Frank looked past the line, seeing neighbors step out of their homes to see the show. *Oh* now *you guys get curious!*

—⁓—

Yes! "It's over," Benz thought in grateful triumph. "You're surrounded. You can't escape."

The Solomons stared out the windows, police lights playing over their faces.

"I told you they'd show up," Stan said, giving his wife a knowing side glance.

"I know, I know," Francine agreed, rolling her eyes.

Oh, enough of this! "It's over!" Benz exploded. "Give up!" She looked to Kate, still reeling from her torture. "Untie me and we can put this behind us!"

"So what happened to our child can happen to someone else's?"

"You're twisting my words!"

"Am I?" Pinpricks of light danced in Francine's irises. "Am I really?"

She's not going to … Benz felt the house shake. *She can't, can she?!*

The pinpricks became shining stars. "We don't think so."

Benz averted her eyes as everything went white.

—⁓—

A massive lightning bolt shot from the clouds, sending Barrow's home up in a terrific explosion. A vicious shock wave dashed everyone against the street, including Frank.

"Uggh!" He found himself on his back, ears ringing as though a prizefighter had laid him out. "Everyone all right?!"

A chorus of weary groans answered.

"Benz!" Getting to his feet, he turned to Barrow's home, seeing only a flaming ruin. "Benz!"

—⁓—

I'm alive. Benz laughed softly. *Ouch, it hurts to laugh!*

26

She reeled from hundreds of aches and pains fighting for her attention. Her neck and stomach hurt, and her knees felt like they were swelling. But it was the sharp pain in her right side that really bothered her. *Might be a cracked rib. Or a broken one.*

Needing something to take her mind off the pain, she looked around the house.

Everything was pulverized, including the floor she was lying on. *How'd they do this so fast?*

The roof was gone, letting in the wind and rain. It was a balm to her wounds, but it made her clothes as heavy as lead blocks.

Benz thought she heard her name being called but couldn't be sure, thanks to the ringing in her ears. But Frank had gotten out.

Wait, was he calling her?

Barrow, she thought. *Where's Barrow? Where are the Solomons?* She saw them standing in what had been Barrow's living room, right next to her on the couch. She was still alive, looking at Benz in a daze.

"Damn," Stan said, looking to Francine. "Why didn't you call the big one?"

"Are you being sarcastic?"

"Glad you caught that."

"I got a little carried away," Francine admitted. "Least I made sure it didn't touch us."

"Yeah, how did you do that?"

"Trade secret," she answered.

"Right," Stan scoffed, rolling his eyes.

They're joking, Benz thought in disbelief. *They destroyed a house—with a lightning bolt—and they're joking about it!* She tried to move, only to stifle a scream as pain shot up her legs. *How do I arrest people that can do that?*

"We didn't have to hurt her," Stan said, gesturing to Benz. "She was nice to us."

"To save *her*," Francine said, stabbing a finger at Kate.

"Right."

Have to do something! Benz thought as she tried crawling toward them. *Have to ... stop them!*

"Well then, Detective," Stan said as Francine yanked Kate to her feet. "It's time for us to go."

"You're hurting innocent people!" *Cripes, Benz! Think of something else!*

"Doesn't seem to stop you guys."

"You won't get away with this," Benz declared. "We *will* stop you." *Somehow.*

"You're welcome to try," Stan said, smiling sadly. "Wish we'd met under … better circumstances."

"Enough talk," Francine cut in, looking skyward. "Let's go."

"Yeah, yeah," Stan agreed, a solemn expression on his face. "Let's go."

Kate thrashed in Francine's grip, her fearful eyes pleading with Benz to do something. Those eyes would haunt her for weeks to come.

All Benz could do was look on helplessly as the Solomons rose off the floor. They never broke eye contact with her until they moved past the ruined house. Search lights fixed on them, revealing their crime—and power—for everyone to see.

Then they shot up into the stormy sky.

We'll … find you, Benz thought, seeing them disappear into angry clouds. *I swear.*

Then she passed out.

—⁂—

"Crap!" Frank cried out as one eye shot open. He tried to sit up, but knives of pain held him fast. A quick glance revealed he was in a hospital room. A nice one, as a matter of fact. *Least I can freak out in style.*

"Frank?" a familiar figure asked, limping toward him.

"Benz!" Frank said as she dragged a chair to his bedside and took a seat.

"Yeah. Glad you're awake."

"Me too. How long have I been here?"

"A few days," Benz answered. "It was touch-and-go during your surgery, but you pulled through okay."

Frank winced at the gaudy bandage on his right shoulder, the same place Stan hit him with his … *Eye beams? Heat vision? God, the world we now live in.* He flexed his arm, found he could move it. He cautiously raised his other hand to a blind side on his face. With relief, he felt a bandage. "And this?"

"You got that when you hit the ground," Benz answered. "Least that's what someone told me."

"I hit the ground?" Frank shook his head in disbelief. "That can't be. I was coming for you."

"I know," Benz said, nodding her head.

"The Solomons had just blown up Barrow's house! I was on my feet and coming to get you!"

"You tripped on debris and fell on your face."

"C'mon! Really?"

"Yup."

"What a letdown."

"I know," Benz said, chuckling humorlessly. "Could've really used you in there."

"I know." Frank looked away from her out of shame and then looked her in the eye. "I'm glad you're alive."

"Me too." But Benz hadn't come away clean. Her left arm was in a cast, the sleeve of her jacket cut to accommodate it. Her lips displayed faint scars, as if they'd been split. Her breathing was labored too, as if her ribs had been cracked.

"I'm sorry I left you behind."

"Frank, I told you to run, remember?" Benz put a warm hand on his shoulder. "Someone had to call for help."

Right, you 'told' me to. "Still, it didn't feel right. Still doesn't."

"Forget it, Frank," Benz said firmly. "It's done."

—◊—

"You keep seeing it in your mind, don't you?" Frank asked after a lengthy silence.

"Hmm?" Benz looked up, shaken out of her musings.

"What happened at Kate's home. What we saw. It shake you up?"

"Yes," she admitted in a mousy squeak. "Yes, it did."

"Yeah." Frank grinned, the gesture looking more like a grimace. "Sure shook me up."

"It was outside our training," Benz declared. "Madsen shouldn't have sent us there."

"I agree."

"So why did he?"

"He was doing his job, Benz."

"Sending detectives to answer a noise complaint? That's a job for patrol officers, Frank. Not detectives like us. We were clear on the other side of town when Madsen called us. At the end of our shift. There are a boatload of other detectives he could've called. Why'd he call us?"

"That was more than a noise complaint, Benz. You know that."

But the junior detective knew she was on to something. "Madsen didn't know that. As far as he was concerned, what Kate had was a simple noise complaint. So why'd he send us?"

"He didn't," Frank answered quietly, staring past her.

"Excuse me?"

"He called me, Benz. You just got dragged along."

"What?" She scooted her seat a little closer to Frank's bedside. "What are you—"

He sighed, leaning back in his bed. "Let's just say I'm a case-closer. The guy he calls when he needs cases solved that are ... out of the ordinary."

Benz cocked her head in confusion. "Surely not like what we just saw!"

"No, but problem cases," Frank clarified quietly. "Cases that might demand alternative solutions."

"Are we talking"—Benz glanced over her shoulder as though she was being watched—"under-the-table stuff?"

"Let's just say not every case can be solved going by the book. Police work doesn't work that way." Frank gave her a sad, resigned smile. "Neither does life."

Benz looked at him in a new light, wondering what he had done in his years on the GCPD. She also wondered whether Madsen would consider her a case-closer like him.

———m———

"So what are we gonna do about the Solomons?"

"Nothing we can do," Frank answered solemnly. "Something tells me it's going to be taken out of our hands." He showed her his palms, as if to emphasize the point.

"Hold on, Frank," Benz said. "We're the primaries on this case!"

"Oh, we'll be asked to put in a report. But that's as far as our involvement's gonna go."

"But ... why?"

"This debacle's an embarrassment. We are too, because we worked it, and everyone knows it. Especially those higher up the food chain. If Madsen's gonna have a chance of salvaging the GCPD's reputation, we can't be seen anywhere near this case."

Benz started to say something, but Frank silenced her with a stern look.

"So what are they going to do?" Benz asked after chewing over *that* revelation. "What can anyone do against power like that?"

"I don't know," Frank answered, his face burning with shame. "I really don't know."

———m———

Excuses, Benz thought, shaking her head in disgust. *Just more excuses. Like acquitting Barrow for shooting Brian or Frank's job as Madsen's cleanup guy. How deep does this crap go?* "What about Kate Barrow? We can't just leave her to them! That's not justice!"

"No, it's not," Frank said, balling his good fist angrily. "But to the higher-ups? This is bigger than her. This is about the GCPD's reputation. That always comes first, no matter what."

I can't believe this, Benz thought, gripping Frank's bedrail. "Are we supposed to act like nothing happened?! Like Kate Barrow and the Solomons don't matter?!"

"No," Frank answered patiently. "We're going to find Kate and the Solomons and bring them in. But not until we're released from here with a clean bill of health."

"Kate could be dead by then, Frank."

"If the Solomons wanted Kate dead, they would've killed her that night. They want her for something else. Until they get it, she'll be fine."

"You don't know that."

"I have to hope, Benz," Frank said quietly. "I have to hope."

SOLOMONS IN THE NIGHT

"Y̶ou wanted to see me, sir?"

"Yes, Inspector," Commissioner Topher Madsen, of the Gateway City Police Department, answered. "Please come in."

Detective Robert Isenguard calmly entered Madsen's office. After closing the door behind him, he took a seat in front of Madsen's desk.

"How do you feel?"

"Fine, sir."

"Good to know," Madsen said, looking older than his fifty years. His once-gunmetal-gray hair had become streaked with white, his once-lively auburn eyes now muted and troubled. It was the result of fielding scathing attacks against the Gateway City Police Department for six months. "How's Drake?"

"Breathing better. But he's a long way from 100 percent."

"He's alive, Isenguard," Madsen stated. "That's more than anyone can say for Kate."

Isenguard caught the bitter way that Madsen referred to the woman whose bullheaded actions had done more to hurt the department than any Internal Affairs probe. *Officer*, he corrected mentally. *She's* still *one of us*. "I still can't believe the Solomons attacked her—in her own home, no less!"

"Back in my day, people knew better than to do that."

"Sir, what if we *never* find her?"

"I don't know." The beleaguered police chief got up from his seat, his button shirt seeming to be hanging from his frame like a loose bedsheet. His posture had stooped, as though he bore the weight of the world on his shoulders. Or, at the very least, the department. "The mayor's calling for my head, and more than a few important people are willing to give it to him."

"Jesus," Isenguard whispered under his breath. "It can't be that bad!"

"It is," Madsen said after letting out a weary sigh, "but there might be some good news."

"I'll take any right now, sir," Isenguard declared, letting out a weary sigh while pursing his lips. "We all could use some." The whole station needed it. At the moment, everyone was either turning in their badges or putting in paperwork for transfer. Or early retirement.

"We might have a way to turn this around."

That is so good to hear! Isenguard smiled. "Knew you'd find a way, sir."

"But I'm gonna need your help."

"Anything you need."

"Good man." Madsen tossed the tall inspector a thin manila folder. "Because I need you for an escort mission."

Isenguard opened it to see a picture of a beautiful Asian woman with a heart-shaped face and short black hair. "Isn't this..."

"Olivia Blaque," Madsen answered after clearing his throat. "Anchor of that show, *Ancient Aliens*."

"I've seen it," Isenguard revealed, looking up from the folder's contents to see Madsen, giving him a confused look. "Francis loves it," he confessed sheepishly. "We watch it together."

"Right." Madsen looked out the window. "Her editor wants footage of the Solomons. In action, believe it or not."

"What for?" Isenguard asked, his brow arching in suspicion. "Stan and Francine aren't aliens."

"After what you read in Drake's report, are you sure?"

On a deserted street, a light flashed. It was so brief that witnesses would have thought nothing of it, but it brought Stan and Francine Solomon back to Gateway City.

—∞—

"What makes Olivia Blaque think her people will catch the Solomons?" Isenguard asked incredulously as he sat in Madsen's office. "They don't exactly pose for autographs!"

"No clue," Madsen answered. "But Mayor Quimby's throwing his weight behind her."

"So, you need me to keep an eye on her team?"

"We can't have them out on their own."

You want everyone to think we're still in control, Isenguard realized darkly.

"We need this to go smoothly," Madsen said, giving the inspector a grim look. "Or things are gonna get a *lot* worse."

Isenguard was momentarily at a loss for words. "How can things get *any* worse?"

"I've heard talk from the district attorney. About department purges. And court hearings."

"You really think it'll go that far?"

"Isenguard," Madsen declared after letting out a regretful sigh, "I'm on the chopping block."

No way. Isenguard blinked in surprise, not sure he heard correctly. "You? Why would …"

"People are saying I offered Kate to the Solomons … to save our skins."

"Like a sacrifice?" Isenguard asked in shock. "Are you kidding me?!"

"Crazy, I know," Madsen said. "But her parents are talking, and people are listening." He paused before adding. "People with influence."

"Aren't people jumping the gun?"

"Since that Solomon kid's shooting—"

"Brian Solomon, sir.

"Huh?"

"His name was Brian Solomon," Isenguard corrected, giving him a slightly disappointed glance. *C'mon, sir, you have to know that! We all have to know that!*

35

"Right. Since his shooting, everyone's equating us with the Klu Klux Klan. That and decades of 'police brutality.'" Madsen rubbed his eyes. "We've lost the people's trust."

"We've lost it before, sir. We always get it back."

"We've never had anyone like Stan and Francine keeping them riled up."

—◆◆—

Olivia Blaque looked over scattered reports of the Solomons on a desk in the hotel she had checked into since arriving at Gateway City.

The one in her hands was from Detective Frank Drake, the first reported witness of the infamous couple using their powers.

A news anchor of ten years, she flipped through the pages, pausing at a picture of Stan and Francine from happier days.

Olivia pulled a picture from her wallet and smiled wistfully. It showed the three of them from their college days.

Now she was a big shot in journalism.

And they were grieving parents turned monsters.

But she would change that.

—◆◆—

In another part of Gateway, two cars engaged in a high-speed chase—the lead car driven by criminals coming from a bank heist, the one hot on its tail a squad car driven by police officers tasked with chasing them. As they swerved around corners, the squad car took heavy fire. Not all the shots hit it, however.

Some hit buildings, sidewalks, and any pedestrian unfortunate enough to be nearby.

Thunder from a sonic boom was all the officers heard as Francine Solomon dropped like a mortar shell on the lead car's hood, stopping it dead in its tracks. But the momentum had to go somewhere. It transferred to the driver and passenger, launching them through the windshield.

The police officers brought their squad car to a screeching halt a few feet from the accident, gawking in horrified shock as Francine floated to the criminals, sprawled and gasping, on the street.

"What do we do?" one of the officers, a rookie named O'Halloran, asked his more experienced partner while remaining frozen in his seat.

"Call it in," his partner, a veteran officer named Murphy, answered, keeping his eyes glued to the improbable scene playing out in front of the bewildered police officers. "Nothing *else* we can do!"

They looked on as Francine grabbed the suspects, gave them a baleful glare, and shot into the sky.

—⋙—

"Hello, Mrs. Blaque," Isenguard said as he met the anchorwoman in one of the station's offices.

"I'd like to thank you for giving us this access," the journalist said, shaking his hand firmly. She was a foot shorter than he was, which was still tall for a woman. Her black hair was cut around her shoulders, her face barely showing a hint of trepidation.

She was dressed in hiking clothes, an apt attire given who she wanted to meet and how. Members of her team—a cameraman, and a photographer—were dressed in similar gear.

"Just three of you?"

"Any more, and we'd call too much attention to ourselves."

She's got common sense, Isenguard thought, relieved. *Hopefully, that'll make this easier.* "Then listen up."

Everyone in Blaque's team turned to face him. "We're going to try to get the Solomons on film. My job—our job," he corrected as he nodded to the chosen officers around him, "is to keep you safe until that happens."

One of Blaque's cameramen raised a hand. "Have they hurt anyone besides—"

"No," Isenguard said, though truth be told, he didn't know. The Solomons hadn't operated long enough to establish a pattern.

"But we're not going to give them reason to," Mrs. Blaque finished. She pointed to one of her cameramen. "Jimmy, keep your camera running. We're not gonna know what footage to use until we get back to the station."

"Copy that, ma'am," he said, nodding his head in understanding.

"Richard," she continued, glancing at the cameraman who had asked the question. "I'm gonna be counting on you for quick shots. Once we see the Solomons, we won't have time to set the scene."

"Yes, ma'am."

"This is your shoot, but it's *my* city," Isenguard cautioned. "In combat situations, *I'm* in command. Is that clear?"

"Crystal," Mrs. Blaque answered, giving him a look of acknowledgment.

"Do what I say when I say it, and we'll be fine."

"Stop where you are!" an irate officer of the GCPD barked in a dingy alley in downtown Gateway City.

"Whoa, whoa, whoa!" a young African American man of about twenty years, dressed in a hoodie and baggy, oversized jeans, answered. Trapped in an alley near Bridge Row, he stood before two officers, hands raised. "I'm not resisting!"

"Stay where you are!" the silver-haired lead police officer bellowed as he and his partner moved in with handcuffs. "HANDS UP!"

"My hands *are* up!" Fearfully, the young man took a step back.

"He's resisting!" the officer said to his partner. "Take him down!"

"Wait, wait!" the man shouted, waving his hands. "Please!"

The other officer was about to move in when four hundred pounds of righteous anger landed in front of him.

"Nice to see things haven't changed," Stan Solomon said as he glared at the two police officers.

"Jesus Christ, no," the lead officer whispered in growing dread. "Not you!"

"Would any *other* black man do?" Stan stepped toward the officers, his eyes ablaze. "Why are you pointing a gun at this man? He's cooperating."

"He's a suspect in our investigation."

"And what proof do you have of this?"

"That's not for you to know."

Stan got in the lead officer's face. "Do you *really* want to spit that bullshit at me?"

"Mr. Solomon, please," the younger officer cut in. "We want to bring him in for questioning. That's all."

"That's not what I heard," Stan said, turning to him, "or what I saw. In fact, it looked like you were about to shoot him." He turned to the older officer, who still had his gun trained on him. "You see why that would bother me."

Understanding the implication, the officer put the gun away.

"Smart man." Stan turned back to the young officer. "What's your name?"

"Jamal," came the uneasy answer. "Jamal Jones."

"Well, Jamal, I know your name and badge number." After a quick glance at the lead officer, Stan continued, "I know your partner's too." His eyes radiated menace. "I find out this man's been mistreated in any way, you both will answer to me."

"Yes, sir. Thank you."

"And that would not be healthy," Stan declared in a no-nonsense voice. "For either of you." With that, he took off into the nighttime sky, leaving the bewildered officers, and the man in the hoodie, staring at each other.

—⚉—

"Here we are," Isenguard declared as he drove the armored transport to a residential neighborhood on the outskirts of Gateway City's business district. "We'll start there."

"This part of the Solomons' territory?" Mrs. Blaque asked, looking out one of the transport's windows with alert eyes.

"We're still figuring that out," Isenguard answered, keeping his eyes peeled for any unwanted surprises.

"There doesn't seem to be any particular place they stick to."

"But?"

"They seem drawn to middle- and low-income neighborhoods."

"Any reason why that is?"

"I'm guessing because those types of neighborhoods remind them of where they used to live," Isenguard answered. He glanced at the back seat to see her cameraman, Richard, filming through the transport's windows while her photo guy, Jimmy, snapped pictures. "You can tell your guys to save their film. We're nowhere near the action yet."

"They're getting establishing shots," Mrs. Blaque explained, "to set up the story."

"This story's not gonna make us look bad, is it?" *Or should I say worse?*

"Any reason it should?" Mrs. Blaque asked, giving the inspector a curious look.

"Do you know the circumstances of Stan and Francine's … creation?"

"We know of the slaying of their son and the officer that did it." Mrs. Blaque paused before continuing. "Speaking of which, I'm sorry to hear about Officer Barrow's abduction."

"Thank you," Isenguard said, giving her a respectful nod. *Glad someone is.*

"And Detective Drake's hospitalization."

Yeah, there's that too. "It's been hard on all of us."

"Maybe our work can help," Mrs. Blaque suggested, her expression brightening, if only for a second.

"How do you figure that?" Isenguard asked, giving the reporter his own curious look.

"If we have the right footage," Mrs. Blaque answered, "it'll show that the Solomons are beyond any law enforcement agency's ability to deal with, let alone apprehend."

"I think the whole city knows that, Mrs. Blaque."

"But no one knows the full extent of their abilities," she explained, her words a patient rebuttal to Isenguard's resigned statement. "The only ones who really know are Detective Drake and Officer Barrow, and we can't exactly reach them for comment."

"What about Detective Benz?" Isenguard asked, giving the shorter woman a wary look. "She was there too. From what I heard, she had a better view of the Solomons' abilities than Drake did."

"Oh, I've tried contacting her," Mrs. Blaque answered, flashing the taller inspector an irritated look. "But she's a hard one to pin down."

You're telling me, Isenguard thought. *Even to her fellow officers.*

Detective Julie Benz was Drake's junior partner, a young woman who had just made detective and had the fire of someone who had something to prove. She wasn't a fan of Kate Barrow, or her not-guilty verdict for killing Brian Solomon.

An opinion she did *not* try to hide, especially around Frank Drake.

Like Drake, she had been put on recovery leave the second GCPD officers pulled her out the wreckage of Kate Barrow's home.

Unlike Drake, she was still able to walk on her own.

Once she was on leave, Chief Madsen put out an order, making Detective Benz off-limits for anyone who wanted to know more about what had happened the night the Solomons kidnapped Kate Barrow.

Even Isenguard was barred from talking to her!

Until the GCPD's union reps were through with her, of course.

"With Benz in the wind," Mrs. Blaque continued, mindless to Isenguard's musings, "all we have to go on is Drake's report."

Wait, what? That snapped Isenguard out of his musing like an air-raid alarm. "Benz made a report too, Mrs. Blaque." *Dammit, Isenguard, you shouldn't have told her that.*

"I know, but your boys in the GCPD won't let my people or me see it." The Asian woman slowly turned her head to look at him from where she sat in the transport. "Do you have it, perchance?"

"Not on me, I'm afraid."

"Can you get it?"

No. Isenguard shook his head, deciding to keep the reporter at a distance. Truth be told, he was sure that if he tried hard enough, he could no doubt get Benz's report. But he had been taught to never trust the media. Not completely. If he got the report to Mrs. Blaque, Isenguard had no doubt that she would either make it public or use it to harass Benz and the GCPD.

Either way, the people closest to the Solomon case would know no peace.

And Isenguard had to put the badge—the GCPD—first.

"Well, since we can't reach Benz's report," Mrs. Blaque said, letting out a resigned sigh as if she knew what Isenguard was thinking, "or Drake's, as far as anyone's concerned, the Solomons are an urban myth, at best." She took a moment to politely clear her throat. "At worst, they're overly competent criminals that your department can't catch."

"A bit disrespectful, but go on," Isenguard said, regretting the GCPD's secrecy, and his desire to participate in it. *All this cloak-and-dagger crap could get people killed.* He actually contemplated getting Benz's report to Blaque just to get the word out. *Madsen has to know that!*

"But if the public got verified footage of the Solomons' powers in action, it would know they're not regular criminals."

"But are something more dangerous," Isenguard reasoned, nodding his head. *That could work!* "Taking the sting of failure off us. I like it. Let's see if you can actually do it."

—m—

Natalie Morgan stood on the ledge of a hotel roof, gazing despondently at a moonlit sky somewhere in Gateway City's hospitality district. She was dressed in a pair of jeans and a T-shirt, a half-empty bottle of bourbon dangling from sweaty fingers.

"Having a bad day?"

"Ahh!" Natalie jumped as Francine Solomon appeared beside her. There had been no hint of her approach. No rustling of the air, no oncoming shadow, nothing. One second, Natalie had been alone, the next, Francine was standing a few feet to her left, looking as though she wanted to be somewhere else. "Holy shit," Natalie whispered, her eyes almost popping out of her inebriated skull, "you're real!"

"Duh," Francine agreed, her cold blue eyes flush with fresh irritation.

"And you're here!"

"You've a gift for stating the obvious."

"That supposed to be a joke?" Natalie asked as she rubbed her bloodshot eyes.

"Life's a joke," Francine answered flatly.

"Heh, and I just got the punchline."

Francine rolled her eyes in exasperation, rubbing the bridge of her nose. "All right, then, out with it. What's your beef?"

"Cancer," Natalie answered after she took another swig of bourbon. "I have cancer."

"What kind?"

"You know the kind that clears up?"

"Yeah," Francine answered, her hard expression softening a little.

"Not *that* kind." Natalie stumbled a bit. "In my spine, liver and lungs."

"Shit," Francine cursed, her voice carrying a touch of sympathy.

"Yeah," Natalie agreed, a pitiful expression flashing across her face. "Doctors say I don't have long."

"You get a second opinion?"

"What do you think I've spent this month doing?"

Francine looked over the edge of the roof, saw a throng of people gathered at the foot of the hotel. She knew the police wouldn't be far behind. "So you've come here to die."

"Bingo," Natalie answered in a voice bereft of hope. "You know how the doctors say I'll look when this cancer takes me?"

"I can imagine."

"Like a corpse," Natalie answered, draining the bottle. "I'll be swimming in my own juices, hooked up to a machine, kept alive in unending pain. Fuck that."

"There might be a cure on the way," Francine said in a solemn voice. "You never know."

"And what if there's not?"

"Good point," Francine admitted, shrugging her shoulders. "So you're here to die on your own terms."

"Damn straight," Natalie answered, nodding her head as the bourbon hit her. "What's the point in going on? You try to do the right thing, and life just ..."

"Spits in your face."

"Exactly," Natalie said, her words slurred.

Francine nodded to the foot of the hotel below them. "Seems like people are trying to help you."

"Those people don't know me," Natalie muttered, waving them off. "Never even heard of me before now. They just like the spectacle."

"No kidding," Francine said, looking impressed by her statement.

"They're here to ease their conscience. They don't care about mine."

As Natalie went on, Francine glanced at a bag to Natalie's left. Left open on its side, it revealed a camera and a picture book, possibly full of photos.

She's an artist. Based on those contents, Francine realized being hooked up to a machine on a hospital bed would kill this young woman way before the cancer did.

"So," Natalie asked after letting the bottle fall from her fingers, "you here to stop me, superhero?"

"On the contrary, I'm here to help you." With that, Francine casually pushed her off the ledge of the hotel. "I'm here to help everyone."

—⚉—

"Everyone, keep your guard up," Isenguard said as their transport arrived at Bridge Row. "This is where the Solomons were last seen. Report everything. Do not fire unless you have my authorization."

The armored transport buckled as it moved. No one dared make a sound.

Bridge Row was a street transformed.

The buildings were twisted spires, red symbols etched into their walls.

The streets had the same markings.

"Looks like they've been"—Olivia swallowed, a knot of dread the size of a plum forming in her throat—"busy." *Stan. Francine.* She kept her hands pressed against a window of the transport to keep them from shaking. *What have the two of you gotten yourselves into?*

"You don't know the half of it," Isenguard said over his shoulder. "All the places they patrol look like this."

Always wanted to be an artist, didn't you, Stan?

Olivia rubbed her eyes to keep them from tearing up. *Stay focused, girl.* "You have any idea what all this is made of?"

"Experts used to flock to our city to sites like this," Isenguard answered while keeping his eyes peeled for threats. "They would even take samples."

There are samples? Olivia looked to the inspector, surprise on her young features. *My editor should've known that! Hell, I should've known that!* "So," she asked, maintaining an amused expression, "what happened to them?"

"They would disintegrate the second they crossed city lines." Isenguard turned his head to look at her. "Kinda surprised you don't know that."

You and me both, Olivia thought ruefully, her jaw clenched in impotent frustration. *Easy, girl. Stay objective.*

But there was no way she could do that, not now. Stan and Francine weren't some random subjects to report on. They were her friends, dammit! Friends that, from the look of things, long since needed her help. "There's no way the Solomons did this on their own,"

"Told my chief the same thing. But that would mean there's more than two of them," Isenguard said in a voice dripping with dread. "He wasn't a fan of that idea."

—⚏—

The streets below the hotel were coming up fast.

Her arms outstretched, as if to embrace the incoming asphalt, Natalie wondered how it came to this, her life reduced to a headline for the tabloids.

She also wondered how her parents would cope. How news of her death would affect her friends.

And what about her plans?

What if a cure could be found?

Did she really want to die?

Oh God, Natalie realized, her breath catching in her throat. *I ... I want to live!* she screamed as the street rose to meet her.

"Oh god, Francine, help me! I want to live! I WANT TO—!" At that moment, Natalie felt something catch her. *Thank you! Thank you! Thank you!*

The knots in her stomach turned to butterflies as her savior coasted them to a roof, away from the hotel and the mob around it. "God, I feel so"—Natalie looked up to see it wasn't Francine who had saved her but her husband—"stupid." *She just left me to die?* She felt a part of herself die at that realization. *Unbelievable!*

"Don't beat yourself up," Stan said in a good-natured voice, taking a step away from her to give her some breathing room.

"Yeah, thanks," Natalie leaned forward, her hands on her knees. Before she could stop it, a wave of vomit erupted from her throat. *Shit!* She kept going, the vomit coming without end. When she finished, she wiped her lips. *That's ... what I get for drinking.* "Sorry," she gasped, looking to Stan, her face flush with embarrassment.

"That's okay," Stan said, his own dark features a mask of sympathy. "Take your time."

"I ... my god!" Natalie instinctively hugged herself. "My body's ... still shaking!"

"It's relieving tension. Don't fight it. It'll pass."

"I ...," Natalie said through chattering teeth, trying to focus her vision on the tall black man standing in front of her. "I ... just need a minute ..."

"Take your time," Stan said in a soothing voice, his hands up in front of her. "Would you like me to hug you? Give you something to lean against?"

"I ... no," Natalie said finally, holding out her hand to keep him from approaching her. "I'm ... I'm fine now," she said, the shakes finally passing. "I'm, I'm better now."

"Good," Stan said with a soothing voice. "Good." He let out a sigh of relief, making a show of wiping at his brow. "Whew! It's a good thing you called out when you did!"

"What? Were you listening for me?"

"Yes, I was," Stan admitted. "I'm always listening, believe it or not. Especially when my wife's out and about."

"So," Natalie said, her embarrassment deepening, "you got to see me chicken out after practically begging Francine to end me. Great. Just freaking great."

"You didn't beg my wife to end your life," Stan said, shaking his head. He paused for a minute. "I didn't mean for that to rhyme."

That actually got a laugh out of Natalie, the statement so out of place, given the situation, that she had no choice but to do so. It was a sad, retched laugh, but one all the same. "God, I feel like such a fool."

"You shouldn't," Stan said, shaking his head slowly. "It took great strength for you to call out for help."

"I sure as hell don't feel strong," Natalie declared, feeling as though she wanted to cry.

"You had the strength to ask for help," Stan said, putting a hand on the young woman's shoulder. "*That*'s strong."

Natalie wanted so much to surrender to that touch. To just melt into Stan's figure for a while, to have him carry the burdens of her life for just a while. *He's married, woman.* "You …" she paused, her eyes watering with tears, "you know I have cancer, right?"

"I can smell it," Stan answered, giving her a sympathetic smile. "You're in the early stages."

"Thanks." A tear rolled down her cheek before she could stop it. *It never gets easier, no matter how many times I hear it.* "You know how doctors treat cancer?!"

"It won't be easy."

"It'll be torture, man!" Natalie shouted, her body shaking with fear.

"If things get too bad," Stan said, placing another hand on her other shoulder, "say my name out loud. No matter where I am in the city, I'll hear it."

"And then what?"

"I'll come. And together, we'll figure something out."

T-that's not good enough! "But—"

Stan held up a hand for her to let him finish. "And if we can't find another way, I'll make sure you die with dignity, okay?"

Natalie felt some of the tension leaving her. She looked up at the man, who was a head taller than she was, her voice coming out a desperate squeak. "You promise?"

"Cross my heart," Stan answered, making a crossing gesture with his hands over his chest. "Now how about you head home? I'm pretty sure there are good people that are worried about you."

"I … I don't live around here."

"In that case," Stan let out an amused sigh, "tell me where you want to go, and I'll fly you there."

"Oh." Natalie blinked in surprise, not believing her luck. "Okay."

—ɷ—

"This is incredible," Mrs. Blaque declared in utter fascination as she stared at the altered streets of Bridge Row from the safety of the armored GCPD transport. "Like something out of a science fiction story!"

"Or a horror story," Isenguard added in a sober voice.

"You read a lot of horror stories, Inspector?" Mrs. Blaque asked, curiously looking over her shoulder at the massive inspector.

Francis sure loves 'em. "I've read my fair share," Isenguard answered in a grim voice, as he kept his hands on the transport's steering wheel. "Particularly of characters going down paths they're not supposed to."

"That's not a ringing endorsement of what we're doing."

"Sorry, Mrs. Blaque," Isenguard said, embarrassed that his dread was showing through. "My spirits aren't exactly high right now."

"Actually," the young woman said. "this supports one of my theories."

Theories? Isenguard's brow arched in skeptical interest. "You got more than one?"

"But of course," Mrs. Blaque answered, giving him a wry smile.

Okay, Isenguard thought, considering her words, *I'll bite.* "Tell me one."

"That the individuals terrorizing your city aren't Stan and Francine at all," Mrs. Blaque answered. "Not really."

"Heh," Isenguard chuckled, trying not to sound rattled. "Then who are they?"

"More like *what* are they."

"Well, what are they?"

"Aliens," Mrs. Blaque answered in a flustered voice, as if understanding how crazy *that* sounded, "or something to that effect, wearing their skins."

Even the most hardened of Isenguard's team, sitting in the back of the transport, perked up at that sentence.

Nice one, Mrs. Blaque, Isenguard thought, seeing hints of nervousness showing on their faces. *As if we weren't scared enough.* But he had kicked off the line of questions, so he had no one to blame but himself. "Care to explain that?"

"No human could erect structures like these so fast," Mrs. Blaque continued, gesturing to the altered neighborhood outside the transport. "They wouldn't have the knowledge."

As they passed another spire, Isenguard saw faces staring out of its windows. *Crap, people live in these things!* They had to be the inhabitants of Bridge Row! Why hadn't they called for help?

"Inspector?"

Stay on mission, pal! Isenguard turned to Mrs. Blaque, his palms sweaty as they gripped the steering wheel. "Mrs. Blaque, the Solomons have powers. Two of those are superstrength *and* speed." *Never thought I'd say* that *with a straight face!*

"Powers don't equate with knowledge," the Asian woman declared wryly, "and it doesn't explain how they're able to create structures like these in a populated city without anyone noticing."

"They could've made them somewhere else and had them brought in."

"Plausible," Mrs. Blaque said, cocking her head in acknowledgment, "but they'd need one hell of a delivery system."

She has a point, Isenguard thought warily, looking from her to the alien-looking streets ahead. *I don't* like that she has a point.

Alan Duke mumbled drunkenly as he drove his truck down the street. In the back was a host of automatic weapons. He kept his eyes focused on the road, looking for that faggot club. "Damn you, Carol," he mumbled as he skidded to a stop at a light. *Not her fault. One of those fucking dykes got to her.* He took a moment to sob, making sure the people in the car next to him didn't see.

It was none of their business.

Besides, they would see the weapons in his truck.

Definitely not their business!

Alan floored the gas when the light turned green, rocketing down the street. *Twenty-seven years*, Alan fumed, growing so angry he could barely see. *Twenty-seven fucking years!* All shot to hell, because Carol got in touch with her inner dyke!

It wasn't fucking fair!

Had she been lying to him the whole time they were married?! Trying to make a fool of him? They had kids, for crying out loud! What would they think when they found out their mother was a dyke?

What would they think of him?

Everyone would think Alan was in on it. That it was his fault. He was the man of the house, after all. "Laughing at me," Alan murmured in a slurred voice. *All of 'em laughing at me. Taking what's rightfully mine. What I worked for! What gives them the right?!*

Alan patted the gun lying on the passenger seat of his truck as he saw the club down the street, playing their faggot music. Club Envy. Jesus Christ, even the name they picked sounded perverted!

I'll make them pay, Alan swore, his sullen eyes on the road ahead of him. He would make them all pay. Every cock-sucking, butt-fucking one of 'em! He would be on the news, maybe even get a spot on *60 Minutes*! "Ruined my family! You won't ruin anyone else's!"

"Well, what do you know?" A baritone voice quipped. "New age, same stupid."

"What the ..." Alan looked to his left, then his right.

He saw no one.

"Hard to believe you can even see with all that booze in your system."

Who the hell's that? Alan realized the voice was coming from under his seat. *Under the truck!* "Who the hell are you?"

"You know what," the baritone voice said, "give me a minute."

A second later, Alan felt his truck rise from the street, and into the air.

Oh fuck! Alan unbuckled his seat belt and reached for the door, only to see that his truck was already too high for him to survive the fall. *Shit, shit, shit!* "Put me down, ya fag!"

"Such language!"

"Who the hell are you?"

"And here I thought I was famous," the voice answered as the truck soared among the clouds. "Let's fix that."

Something ripped Alan's driver-side door away.

"Fuck!" Alan cursed; his eyes wide with fear at the dark shape on the other side of the door. A massive black hand grabbed him, yanking him into the brisk, frigid air.

"Oh my god, it's you!" Alan whispered as he found himself face-to-face with the infamous Stan Solomon. "Please, let me go! I … I didn't kill your kid!"

"Never said you did," Stan said, his voice going from cordial to acidic. "But you were going to kill other people's kids. Kids with families. Parents who don't deserve the pain of burying their own." He leaned in close, his eyes blazing like crimson floodlights. "You can see why that would bother me."

"You're supposed to be on our side!"

"I may be on the side of the people," Stan answered as he held Alan in one hand and his truck in another, like it was a mere basketball, "but I will never be on the side of *your* people."

One of 'em, Alan thought, his jaw quivering in horrified disbelief. *He's fucking one of those damn faggots, down below! Why else would he be helpin' 'em?!*

"I think it's time you went on a little trip," Stan declared, as if hearing his words. "After you tell me who sold you the guns, you got in your truck, here."

"I'll never talk," Alan snarled, trying to remain brave in Stan's vice grip. "Not even if you torture me!"

"So many people say that," Stan stated, looking amused. "Until the torture starts."

"Oh no," Alan whimpered as he watched Stan reduce the truck to slag, simply by looking at it with his red-hot heat vision. "Please, man! Let me go! I haven't hurt anybody!"

"You were going to."

"But I didn't! You stopped me before I could, okay? Lesson learned! I'll never hurt anyone!" Alan raised a trembling hand as though he was swearing on a stack of bibles. It was so hard for him to do, what with frigid winds nipping at his skin. "Scout's honor!"

"I've heard promises like that *so* many times," Stan said as he let the molten metal that had been Alan's truck fall from his fingers to the ground, hundreds of feet below. "Only to see the same crimes committed by the same people who should know better." He looked to the horizon, seeing the moon shining in the distance. "Not this time."

"Oh God, please!" Alan begged, breaking into a sob as the winds went from frigid to downright artic, painfully stinging the skin of his face. "I … I have kids!"

"You should've thought about them before you came out ready to kill," Stan stated coldly as he glared at the blubbering man. "But hey, don't fret."

"Huh?" Alan blinked, a hopeful expression on his face. "Why?"

"They'll still have their mother."

—⟊—

"We need to collect samples."

I had a sinking feeling she'd say that, Isenguard thought, giving her an annoyed look from the transport driver's seat. "This isn't a safari, Mrs. Blaque."

"If we don't bring back physical proof of what we're seeing," the young reporter declared from her seat behind the inspector, "our report's not gonna make a difference. It'll be dismissed as simple science fiction."

Thought the footage was *the physical proof,* Isenguard thought, his lips becoming a firm line on his face. But as much as he hated to admit it, he saw the logic in Mrs. Blaque's words. Keeping his expression professional, he turned to his men sitting in the back of the transport, alongside Mrs. Blaque and her cameramen. "What do you say, boys? Up for a walk?"

"Fine with us, sir," one answered as the others nodded in agreement.

"All right, then." Isenguard coasted the transport to a stop at a nearby curb and put down the brake. "Let's take a walk."

—⟊—

Stan? Francine? I'm here, Olivia thought as she stepped out of the transport and onto an alien world. *Where are you?*

The air smelled strange and tasted stranger on her lips. The Asian woman knelt down, ran a delicate hand along the surface of the street. "This feels warm." Olivia felt the heat radiating through her fingers and up her arm. "How long's this been going on?"

"Street's been altered for months now," Isenguard answered, watching the rooftops of buildings around them, like the rest of his men were doing. "This is the first time it's ever been warm."

"Have you felt it yourself?"

"No way." He shook his head vigorously. "I'll leave that to you, thank you very much."

Olivia couldn't blame him for his hesitation. It was one thing to transport buildings from one place to another, but to alter a city's very nature without anyone knowing?

Right under their noses?

That took not just inhuman intelligence but speed too. And an incredible amount of resources.

—◊—

Stan and Francine met high in the nighttime sky, sharing a hungry, passionate kiss.

"I missed you," Stan declared, a groan of desire rumbling in his throat. "Did you miss me?"

"We've only been apart for a few hours," Francine giggled, her cheeks burning with embarrassment.

"I know, but the longer I'm away from you, the more unbearable it feels."

She gave her husband a worried look. "You don't think that's from what happened to us, do you?"

"I hope not," Stan answered, his expression becoming stern. "Speaking of which …"

"Funny," Francine said in a sarcastic voice. "I can feel the argument before you even start."

"I ran into one of your 'attempts' tonight."

"How nice," she said in a slightly bored tone.

"In fact," Stan added sarcastically, "I saved her from going splat on the pavement."

"Oh," Francine said, examining her nails as though she didn't care. "She didn't land? How about that?"

"Care to explain what you were thinking?"

"About the woman with cancer?"

"Yes, Frannie," Stan continued in a strained voice, "the woman with cancer."

"I gave her what she wanted," Francine said, casually shrugging her shoulders. "She should be thanking me."

"You almost killed her," Stam declared, holding her in his arms so she couldn't escape. "Why would you even think of doing that?"

"She wanted to die, Stan."

"I don't doubt that," Stan stated with forced patience, "but you could've talked her out of it."

"You mean the way everyone tried to talk *us* out of getting justice for Brian?" Francine hissed, giving him a hard look.

"You can't keep diverting every discussion we have to that."

"She didn't want to live," Francine said, shrugging her shoulders again as though what they were talking about was no big deal. "All I did was skip the middleman."

"And what if I hadn't been there?"

"Then her suffering would've been over."

"Such a hopeful person you are," Stan uttered, rolling his eyes while letting out a resigned sigh.

"I heard you, by the way," Francine said, looking at him with disgusted eyes.

"Oh, did you?" Stan asked, arching his brow in shock. "How close were you?"

"Close enough."

"Close enough to hear that young woman crying out for someone to save her?"

"Yeah," Francine answered, not even denying it. She floated out of Stan's embrace then started circling her husband. "I did."

"Why didn't you save her?"

"Because she *wanted* to die, Stan!" Francine insisted in a frustrated voice. "I simply gave her what she wanted. And forced her to live with her decision! And she would have, until you saved her! And worst of all, you started talking to her like some freaking cult leader!"

"I fortified her spirit," Stan declared in a defensive voice. "I'm not going to apologize for that."

"You gave that poor woman a hope you can't live up to," Francine snapped, her lips twisting in disgust. "That'll do more damage to her than the cancer."

"You don't know that," Stan insisted in a patient yet irritated voice.

"At least my way, she would've gone out on her own terms. Now she'll be a victim of charlatans using her desperation to line their pockets."

"Then we'll have to make sure that doesn't happen," Stan declared in an exasperated voice while gently massaging the bridge of his nose for strength. "That's why we're here."

"But it's not the only reason we're here," Francine insisted, raising an uncompromising finger to his face. "Don't forget that!"

—⁂—

"So you're an expert on the Solomons," Isenguard said as he led his party—consisting of a GCPD officer, Mrs. Blaque, and her cameramen—through Bridge Row's deserted streets. *Can't believe you got me and my people out in the open like this!* He eyed the rooftops of structures and buildings looming over them from opposite sides of the street. *Such a bad idea!*

But Blaque's interest—or was it desperation—to learn more about the environment that Bridge Row had become had pushed him to undisciplined action. He just had to hope that wouldn't bite him and his people in the ass later.

"I like to think so," Mrs. Blaque answered as she followed a step behind Isenguard, snapping him out of his musings. "But really, who is?"

This seems like more than journalistic curiosity, Isenguard thought, his lips turning up in a frown. "How long have you been studying them?"

"About a year." She noticed the look Isenguard gave her. "You seem perplexed."

She catches on quick, Isenguard thought, turning to give the Asian woman a suspicious glance. "You just seem more … knowledgeable of the Solomons than most journalists I've met,"

"And how many journalists have you met, Inspector?"

"More than a few," Isenguard answered, turning his eyes back to the rooftops around him and his party. "More than a few."

——✦——

He suspects me of having an ulterior motive, Olivia realized as she kept an eye on the oversized inspector. *I can hear it in his voice.* She pressed her lips together in grim decision. *I'm gonna have to keep an eye on that.*

From what she had heard about the GCPD, from reliable sources of course, suspicion was more trusted than fact.

It wasn't that Olivia feared that Isenguard would pull a gun on her.

But she knew that if Isenguard suspected, even for a second, what her real goal was, he would pull her and her cameramen out of the Bridge Row so fast her head would spin.

And Olivia couldn't let that happen.

Not until she was sure that her theory about Stan and Francine was correct.

——✦——

"Believe me," Stan said, focusing on his wife's face and not on the waving finger in his face. "I haven't forgotten."

"Good," Francine said, looking relieved while lowering her finger.

"But what's the point of having these powers," Stan asked, giving her an earnest look, "if we don't use them to help people?"

"What's the point in helping people," she countered quickly, "if they don't deserve it?"

Dammit, Francine. Stan sighed, keeping his tone as calm as he could. "You can't keep punishing the city for the crime of one cop." *You used to be a teacher. You should know this!*

"Even if the city acquitted her of the crime?"

What's happened to you, Francine? Stan thought, giving his wife a sad look. *What's happening to us?* "Baby, Kate Barrow can't hurt us anymore."

"She already has," Francine said solemnly, giving him a bitter, regretful look while her shoulders wilted with sadness.

"And she paid for that," Stan said as he pulled her close to him for a loving embrace. "Remember?"

—◊◊—

"Of all the structures we've passed on Bridge Row," Isenguard declared as he, Olivia, and his team, approached a particularly interesting spire in the middle of an intersection of four streets, "this one's special."

"Yes, it is," Olivia agreed heartily, looking up, and up, and up the structure. She saw, to her surprise, that it was bigger than the others, draped in white, its symbols black instead of red. "This must be the Solomons' home. Or perhaps, an entrance to their home!"

"That reverence I hear in your voice?" Isenguard asked, giving her a suspicious look.

"Just admiring their handiwork, Inspector."

"Just remember the monsters that made it."

Monsters your *people created*, Olivia thought dismissively. "Jimmy," she said, turning to one of her cameramen, "get a shot of this. A sweeping shot, then pan wide."

"No problem, Mrs. Blaque," the young cameraman answered as he took his position.

"Richard, I want snapshots of the symbols," Olivia commanded, pointing to her other cameraman. "Get as many as you can. Don't get too close."

"No problem, Mrs. Blaque," he answered as he tentatively approached the spire.

"What are you gonna do with the pictures?" Isenguard asked in a particularly suspicious voice.

"Get them to a linguist," Olivia answered. "They may be part of a language."

"What makes you think they're not just decoration?"

"They might just be, but I'm hoping they're more than that," Olivia answered, doing her best to keep the desperation out of her voice. "If the Solomons are merely aliens, wearing Stan and Francine's skins, as I mentioned to you earlier, these symbols might be the key to communicating with them."

"Or the beings that created them," Isenguard added, giving the skies a wary look. "Not sure that's a good idea."

—❦—

"And you know what? Speaking of making the right people pay for their actions," Stan said, cradling Francine in his arms as they hovered high in the skies above Gateway City, "I got you a present."

"A present?" she asked, her eyes sparkling with interest. "What kind of present?"

"The kind I think you're gonna like," Stan answered, letting go of her and lowering himself down to the city skyline. "C'mon!"

"Stan," Francine said, following behind him, "if you're messing with me ..."

"Since when have I ever messed with you when it comes to getting a present?" Stan asked, hoping this would brighten his wife's dour mood. As he touched down on a nearby building's rooftop, he took a quick listen just to make sure his wife's present hadn't gone anywhere.

Thankfully, it was right where he had left it.

"Okay," Francine said, landing silently on the rooftop, wearing an expression of anticipation. "I'm here. Where's my present?"

"Right here," Stan said, reaching his arm behind the building's thick brick chimney to roughly pull a disheveled middle-aged man, wrapped in metal piping, into view.

"I ..." Francine blinked, giving the man a curious once-over. "Stan? Who is this man?"

"This, my dear, is Alan Duke," he answered, stepping to the side of him to give Francine a better look. "A true example of the hidden hatreds of the people in this town."

Francine slowly approached the unconscious Alan Duke, her eyes going over him in a quick examination. She touched his head, gently turning it from one side to another. "Looks a little worked over. What happened to him?"

"I ran into him," Stan said, puffing his chest proudly, "driving to a nearby nightclub, intending to commit a hate crime."

"Oh, did you?"

"Oh yeah," he answered, nodding. "He was gunning his truck, loaded with guns that I'll bet weren't registered, to a gay nightclub that opened a few weeks ago."

Francine's eyes went wide with shock and indignation. "Club Envy?"

"That's the one."

"Well, I'll be." Francine's eyes went from Stan back to Alan. "Why's he knocked out?"

"Well, I took him up for a ride in the clouds. Turned his truck and those guns to slag with my powers." Stan shrugged his shoulders, as if what he had just said wasn't a big deal. "Guess seeing all that was too much for him."

"Good lord, Stan," Francine said, looking from Alan to her husband, "you gotta prepare folks for something like that! You could've killed this man from shock alone!"

"I don't care about the 'welfare' of shooters, Francine," Stan declared, giving her a grim look. "Especially narrow-minded assholes intending to open fire on a group of people who have the right to feel safe to be themselves." He leaned closer, catching his wife's eye. "And I know you have a kinship with the people who frequent that club."

Francine did a surprised double take, then silently nodded her head. "You're right." She touched Stan's arm, finding the muscles tensing up under the fabric of his suit. "You did good, honey. You did real good."

"Thank you," he said, allowing his muscles to relax. "Do you feel better?"

"You know what," she said after taking a moment to think about it, "I do."

"Good," Stan said, letting out a sigh of relief. "Then meeting this guy," he said, jabbing a finger at Alan, "was worth it for that alone. Not to mention the terrible tragedy I averted."

"You're too good to me," Francine declared, her eyes brimming with adoration as she gazed upon her husband.

"Well, you make it easy," he said, giving her a proud smile. "Some days are easier than others—"

"What's say we get this piece of scum back to our home," Francine said quickly, "so we can find out who sold him those guns?!"

"And then pay that person a visit?"

"Yes, baby," Francine answered, getting on tiptoe to give Stan a kiss on the cheek.

"Sounds good to me," Stan said, wrapping an arm around Alan's chest and rising into the air.

Smiling like a cat that had swallowed a canary, Francine rose with him.

—⚊—

The Solomons gotta be close. We're in their backyard—they GOT to be close! Isenguard turned to one of his operatives holding a scanner up to the skies. "Anything?"

"Nothing yet."

"Copy that," Isenguard said, working hard to keep the creeping worry out of his voice. "Keep me apprised, and if you pick up anything, don't keep it yourself."

"No worries on *that*, sir," the operative agreed, giving him a nod of agreement.

We're in the backyard.

Isenguard shivered as he imagined running into the Solomons, recalling the macabre details of Drake's and Benz's reports of what the Solomons did to them.

Drake's in intensive care, and Benz is on leave, her mind besieged by nightmares, he thought, finding himself stoking his gun for some sense of reassurance. *That could be me. That could be all of us if we're not careful.*

Isenguard's men did the same, all the while keeping their eyes on the skies.

It was bad enough they were in the Solomons' territory, but at least they'd had the security of the transport before. Now they were out in the open.

Get a hold of yourself, Isenguard said to himself. "I know we're scared, boys, but remember our training. We'll get through this."

"Didn't Drake and Benz think the same thing?" one of his officers asked.

"They didn't have backup," another answered, "or the best in police weaponry."

"Think that'll matter?"

We need to keep moving. Isenguard turned to Mrs. Blaque, flashing her an impatient look. "Do you have what you need?" PLEASE *say you have what you need!*

"Almost," she answered patiently. "Just need a few more minutes."

"A few more—" Isenguard's eyes widened when he saw her tapping the spire's wall. "What the hell are you doing?!"

"Seeing if there's a door."

"Seeing if—," Isenguard started, then stopped, doing a surprised double take. "A door?! What the hell for?!"

"So we can get inside," Mrs. Blaque answered, looking at the inspector as though *he* had the problem.

Why the hell would she want to get inside?! "Get away from there!" Isenguard bellowed, taking an angry step toward her. "Now!"

"We're not going to get answers if we stay out here," she insisted, feeling around the surface of the spire as though she knew what she was doing. "And I need answers!"

You need... Isenguard approached quickly, his eyes staring daggers. "I knew there was more to this than professional curiosity! Tell me why you're really here! Right now!"

—⁓—

Stan and Francine watched from the clouds above Gateway City, their eyes zeroing in on the police, slithering around the entrance to their home, which had somehow appeared in Bridge Row.

How long have they been there? Stan wondered, his mouth agape in shock. *And how'd they find it? A better question, what's it still doing here?! It should've disappeared the second Frannie and I left its walls!*

"Is that Olivia?" Francine asked in surprise, squinting for a better view.

Is it? Stan telescoped his vision on three people *not* in police uniform. *It is Olivia! Well, how about that?* "Huh. Haven't seen her since college."

"Got to be looking for a story," Francine said in a suspicious voice. "She's a journalist now."

"If you call the History Channel journalism."

Francine frowned, looking at her husband. "You used to love the History Channel!"

"I used to love a lot of things," Stan declared, a faraway look in his eyes.

"Thank you, Mr. Drama," Francine muttered, giving him an irritated side glance. "We got a real problem here. We can't go anywhere near our home until those police officers leave."

"I'm more concerned about how they found our home," Stan stated grimly.

"Right now, our main concern is gonna be making them leave."

—◊◊◊—

Dammit, I showed my hand too soon. Olivia clenched her jaw, cursing herself for her impatience. She turned to face Isenguard, her hands raised, feeling like a matador facing an oncoming bull. "Calm down, Inspector."

"Why are you really here?" the big man demanded as he approached her. "Tell me!"

Olivia was about to answer when thunder wrenched her gaze upward. "Shit."

"They're close," one of Isenguard's officers stated. "Real close!"

"Where are they?" another asked frantically. "Just tell me where they are!"

"Right here," Francine Solomon whispered, swooping down on them like a vulture from the skies.

—◊◊◊—

So here you are! Isenguard thought as he looked at one-half of a couple that had bedeviled his home for over a year. *Thought you'd look scarier!*

The figure Drake described in his report was a rabid dog, frothing at the mouth. The figure in front of him was a curvy woman, with porcelain skin and a wicked smile. If not for her fiery red hair, he would've mistaken her for an albino. That and the blue eyes.

Where'd Stan meet you? Isenguard wondered, momentarily captivated by her beauty. Her face was too bewitching for her to be a native. Not that the women in Gateway City were ugly, but Francine was something else!

She was dressed in a full bodysuit, like in those comic book movies, with a cape flapping behind her. There was no zipper or anything that hinted at how she took it off.

Maybe she couldn't take it off.

Isenguard's eyes, in the few seconds between registering her presence and prepping for her attack, zeroed in on the symbol on her chest.

Stan's a breast man, it seemed. Man after my own heart!

The symbol was of a firebird, wings outstretched, wingtips touching her shoulders. Francine's ruby-red lips completed the image as they twisted into a smile.

It made Isenguard think of blood.

—⟋⟍—

I'll say this much, Frannie, Olivia thought, her heart skipping a beat as Francine's eyes darted from one member of Isenguard's team to another, *you can still stop traffic, just like you did in college!*

"Liv!" Richard hollered from across the street. "Snap out of it!"

Right, she thought, shaking out of her momentary stupor. *Still got an effect on me too!*

—⟋⟍—

Still takes your breath away, doesn't she, Liv? Stan thought, catching Olivia's reaction to Francine's arrival. *Mine too.* His mind flashed back to the day he first met Francine.

He, on leave after his first deployment.

She, alone and irresistible, at the far end of the bar.

All it took was a stray glance they both shared. And Stan knew he had found the woman he would spend the rest of his life with.

—◊◊—

Moving quickly, Isenguard dropped to one knee and fired at Francine, aiming for her knees. It bought his team a few seconds, knocking her feet out from under her. He was about to bark an order when white light washed over everything. He saw, to his surprise, that the tower's doors were opening!

—◊◊—

It's opening! Olivia thought excitedly. *The tower's opening!*

Richard and Jimmy stood by her side, having run from across the street, all the while dodging gunfire. "What's the plan, boss?!"

Olivia cocked her head toward the light. "We go in!"

Both men grimly nodded, determination on their faces. "Then let's do it!"

—◊◊—

Did Olivia just run into our house?! Stan thought in shock as he hovered fifty feet over Bridge Row. His position afforded him a bird's-eye view of Francine battling the GCPD's officers. It was the only reason he was able to see Olivia and her people running into their home. He was so surprised he almost dropped Alan Duke, who he had been holding since he caught him a few blocks away.

And she's bringing people with her? What is she planning?

"Get her!" Francine shouted from the street.

I am not *leaving you alone!*

"What about you?!"

"I'll be fine! We can't let Liv see what's inside!" she bellowed before turning to the officers marshalling around her. "Now get going!"

Dammit, you're right. Stan shot from the sky, straight through the door of their tower, and deep into the heart of their fortress.

—⚭—

This wasn't supposed to happen, Isenguard thought as talons of panic gripped his beating heart. "Fall back to the transport!" He threw a glance at the officers, marshalling close to Francine. "Lay down cover fire!"

—⚭—

Inside Stan and Francine's lair, Olivia felt like a rat running through a maze.

There were too many details for her mind to process, the colors pinging off the walls playing havoc with her eyes. What little her brain could put together told her she was seeing computers, but more alien than any she had ever seen.

—⚭—

"Isenguard!" Chief Madsen barked from the transport's radio. "What's happening?"

"We're in trouble!" he shouted back as he frantically reloaded his weapon while taking quick looks out of the transport's windows.

"Isenguard," Madsen said in a worried voice, no doubt from the sounds of gunfire, going on around the giant detective, "what *kind* of trouble?"

"Solomon trouble, sir!"

"Goddammit, Isenguard!" Madsen cursed, the sound of something breaking punctuating the anger in his words. "That wasn't the objective!"

"I know, sir!" Isenguard shouted, wincing at the gunfire around him. "Blaque's gone off script!"

"Where's she, now?"

"In their tower!"

"They have a tower now?!" Madsen shouted in disbelief. "How the hell do they have a tower?!"

Stop yelling at me, you freaking son of a bitch! Isenguard mentally counted to ten, struggling to hold his anger in check. "I don't know, sir! They just do, now!"

"What about the footage Blaque was working on?"

"I don't know, sir," Isenguard answered. "She's on her own program!"

"Goddammit!"

"We need backup, now!"

"It's on the way," Madsen said hopefully, already moving to mobilize reinforcements. "Just dig in and stay alive!"

—៣—

Stan flew through their tower like a shark on the hunt, Alan Duke weakly struggling in his grip. *Where the hell's Olivia? She can't have gotten far!*

—៣—

C'mon, big girl! Isenguard stepped out of the transport, firing on Francine.

Let's see what you're packing in that body of yours!

Her eyes locked on to him like daggers as bullets bounced off her face, like kernels of popcorn against a metal wall.

Shit!

Isenguard had only a second to drop out of the way of Francine's fist as it went through the transport's passenger-side door!

Turns out you're packing a lot!

—៣—

At last, here we are, Olivia thought, coming upon a room with vaulted ceilings. The same symbols decorated the walls, making her eyes hurt. But that wasn't what told her she was in the right place.

It was the large eye looking from the ceiling, veiny wires extending from it to every computer screen in the room.

This is the heart of the place, Olivia realized, looking at all of it in awe. *Or it's brain!*

"Okay, we're here," Richard stated quickly as Jimmy took point. "Now what?"

Olivia was about to answer when something big slammed into the three of them from the tower's doors.

—⁓—

She could kill all of us with a blink, Isenguard thought as he dodged another blow from Francine. *So why isn't she?*

He glanced over his shoulder at the open tower doors.

Of course! Blaque and her people are still inside!

He ran for the spire's doors, only for Francine to knock him back with a simple back-handed slap.

"Not for you," she said as he bounced across the ground. "Though you're free to leave."

"Not … without"—*Don't pass out*, Isenguard said to himself—"our people!"

"Indignant until the end." Francine grinned, looking impressed. "I can work with that."

—⁓—

Blinking stars from her eyes, Olivia hoisted herself painfully to her feet. She turned to see Richard and Jimmy on the floor, out cold. She also saw what hit them.

Or more accurately, *who* hit them.

What the … Olivia wondered, seeing an older man on top of them. *Where'd you come from?*

"Alan Duke," a familiar voice echoed. "A true specimen of this city."

Olivia's eyes fastened onto Stan, floating at the room's entrance. Clothed in a dark bodysuit with fiery red eyes, he looked more like a mythic god than the sweet jock she met in college. "Someone's leveled up."

"Always with the jokes. Even when you're sticking your neck where it doesn't belong."

—⚭—

You cold-blooded, little–! Isenguard thought as he struggled to get to his feet. "Is she alive?"

"Who?" Francine asked, though it was clear from her smirk she knew who he was talking about.

"Kate Barrow!" Isenguard answered heatedly. "Is she alive?!"

"Yeah," she answered, her smirk breaking into a grin, "more or less."

"Whatever you do to this city, it won't bring your son back."

"Oh, I know," Francine declared as her expression hardened. She grabbed Isenguard by the throat, lifting him off the ground with one hand. "But it'll keep you joy-boys from killing someone else's. I'll take comfort in that."

—⚭—

"Let me tell your story," Olivia blurted out, hoping to buy herself time until she thought of a better plan.

"Same old Liv," Stan snickered. "Fishing for a headline."

"Someone's going to eventually," Olivia continued, eyeing the way Jimmy and Richard weren't moving. "It might as well be me."

"What makes you think I'll tell you anything?"

"Because we're college buddies."

"Not that you bothered to keep up with us," Stan said, giving her a cold look.

"I'm sorry about that," Olivia said with genuine empathy, "and about what happened to Brian."

Stan winced as though he had been slapped. "Should've known you'd find out about that."

"It made national news."

"I know," he said, shaking his head sadly. "Still can't believe that."

"The riots did too," Olivia added. "Did you know fifty-five people died?"

"Wasn't on my list of priorities," Stan said, showing discomfort. "I had a wife to help through her grief."

"Was it her idea? Getting powers? Going after Kate Barrow?" She gestured to the tech around them. "All this?"

"Are you turning this into an interview?"

"If it'll help, yes."

—⁓—

"All I have to do is say the word," Isenguard warned as he glared at Francine.

"And your people will fire?" she answered in a mocking voice. "That'll hurt you more than me."

"You sure about that?"

"I'm willing to try it if you are."

Damn, Isenguard thought, cursing to himself. What made him think he could bluff her?

"And about that backup your chief promised you?" Francine added, her voice dripping with superiority. "I wouldn't hold my breath."

"You got good ears," Isenguard said in casual voice, implying a bravado he didn't feel. *There's nothing in the files about the Solomons having super hearing! What other powers do they have?!*

"Nothing enters or leaves unless we allow it," Francine explained, clearly emboldened by his discomfort. "Why do you think you got this far?"

Dang it, Isenguard cursed mentally. "You knew we were here the whole time."

"You're not exactly the marines, Inspector Isenguard."

—⁓—

"How'd you do it?" Olivia persisted, taking a step toward Stan, her eyes alight with a spark of interest. *Keep him talking, girl!* "The spires, the streets, everything?! How'd you do it?!"

"We have our ways," Stan answered, folding his arms authoritatively.

"You and Francine have only had your powers for a short while," Olivia pressed. "No way you had time to alter the city this much, this fast. Not by yourselves."

Stan stayed silent.

Because it wasn't by yourselves. "You didn't come back alone, did you?"

"Not this time," Stan answered as the giant eye above them crackled with electricity.

Olivia looked up, seeing the ceiling part, strange creatures descending toward them.

—⟋⟍—

Francine made a show of releasing her grip on Isenguard's throat.

Oh, you horse-humping—his mind got out before he hit the ground—*cunt!*

"Well? C'mon, then," she said, turning to the officers surrounding her. "Let's get on with it!"

"Hold your fire!" Isenguard wheezed painfully. But his throat hurt so much he couldn't get his words above a whisper.

So his people opened fire.

—⟋⟍—

"Hold up," Olivia said as the creatures came into view. "What are—"

"Our helpers," Stan answered as they moved through the room. "Loyal only to us."

They looked like oversized jellyfish, with a long curved "shell" as a main body and multiple tentacles underneath. They were white, like the fortress, but their tentacles varied from dark black to light gray, maybe hinting at different functions. Each shell displayed the same mark that was on the walls of the Solomons' tower.

Olivia watched the robots' tentacles swarm Alan Duke, lifting him from Richard and Jimmy, who were finally waking up. "Where are they taking him?"

"To his punishment," Stan answered, watching as his robots lifted a kicking and screaming Alan Davis into the ceiling of the room. The ceiling's doors cut off his screams as they closed behind him. "As I promised."

My theory was right, Olivia realized as she saw the means Stan and Francine used to alter Gateway City so fast. *Hope I get to tell someone.*

—⁂—

No!

Isenguard looked on in horror as Francine cut his people down as though they were nothing. He winced as a sharp pain in his side flared up. It had to be a broken rib. Maybe more.

I can't just lie here!

He shakily pulled a pistol from his vest as Francine whittled his team down to three. *Please let this work.* He forced his fingers to pull the trigger. *Now!*

He fired, the round hitting Francine on the side of her head. It staggered her for a second, giving his people time to get the wounded to the transport.

"You son of a—" Francine whirled on him, wearing a smoking dent in her head and a mask of rage that promised legendary heights of suffering to come.

—⁂—

What to do? Stan floated over Liv and her crew. *How to end this?*

A backhand slap could take their heads off their shoulders; they wouldn't even feel it. A heated glare could flash-fry them; they wouldn't even need coffins.

"Stan?" Olivia asked, a timbre of worry in her voice. "Talk to me, here."

She was afraid of him. They said that would happen. People in power always fear people with more power. Stan knew those people had sent Liv and her cameramen to fall on the sword for them. They were too cowardly to take the risk themselves. If he killed Olivia and her people, they would benefit, and there was no way he was gonna let that happen.

"Stan?" Olivia asked, looking like a kid worrying over their parents' reaction to a bad grade on a report card. "What are you thinking?"

"Coming to a decision," he answered, a decisive expression coming to his face. "Here's what we're going to do."

—៣—

Francine was about to crush Isenguard's face in her hands when her brow arched in surprise. "No way."

No way what? Isenguard wondered wearily, his boy hanging from her grip like a puppet with its strings cut. *What's happening?*

"No freaking way!" Francine bellowed, whirling on the tower. "You've *got* to be kidding me!"

What, dammit? Looking up, Isenguard saw Stan Solomon floating out of the tower's doors, Olivia Blaque and her cameramen walking cowed behind him.

"Francine," he declared in a voice that brooked no argument. "It's time to go."

She looked back at Isenguard, still in her grip. "This is a mistake."

"If it is," Stan said, glancing at Mrs. Blaque, "we know where she lives."

"That we do." Francine floated toward her husband, passing Blaque and her people as they walked to Isenguard in a parody of a hostage exchange.

Blaque didn't look right. Her eyes were red, enflamed, as though she had stared into the sun.

"What happened in there?" Isenguard demanded as he staggered to his feet.

"We got what we needed," the reporter mumbled, holding a thumb drive in her hands. "We need to go."

"What was the point of all this?" Isenguard gestured angrily to the devastation around them. "What was the freaking point?!"

"You want answers, talk to your boss," Francine answered dismissively. "He's used to making all sorts of dirty deals."

What's that *supposed to mean?!* Isenguard's eyes widened in incredulous wonder. *What do they know?!*

"Tell me, Inspector," Stan said, turning his gaze on him. "While you were here, how many criminals were left unattended? How many innocents suffered because of that?"

"That's not for you to decide," Isenguard declared, glaring at the caped man.

"And that dumbass statement," Francine declared, floating next to her husband, "is why we're here."

"That a threat?"

"No," Stan answered as they receded behind the tower's doors. "It's a promise."

"We're not going anywhere," Francine added as their tower faded before everyone's eyes. "Might as well get used to it."

Olivia sat in interrogation at the GCPD an hour later, waiting for her lawyer.

Isenguard took her there, right after he and what was left of his team left Bridge Row. She didn't even have time to make sure Jimmy and Richard were okay.

Olivia glanced at the mirror across from her, knowing Chief Madsen and his cronies were looking at her from the other side. Observing her like an animal in a cage, waiting for her to break.

Keep waiting. She nonchalantly scratched an itch in the small of her back. *I've been through worse.*

"Isenguard," Madsen said, his arms crossed in disapproval as he stared at Mr. Blaque from the other side of the one-way mirror. "What were you thinking bringing her here?"

"I want to talk to her, Chief," Isenguard answered, standing next to him.

"We can't hold her, Isenguard."

"I know," the oversized inspector admitted. "That's not the point."

"Then what *is* the point?" Madsen asked, his patience wearing thin. "Why'd you bring her here?"

"Did you read my report?"

"I did," Madsen answered, massaging the bridge of his nose, "and there's no evidence to suggest she's working with the Solomons."

"She didn't come to Gateway City just to get footage of them," Isenguard insisted. "I looked up her file, sir. She knew them from college. Shows a prior relationship, maybe even a bias."

"It's not enough to charge her."

"I don't want to charge her. I just want to work her for information before her lawyer comes for her."

"Her lawyer's already here," Madsen declared, cocking a glance at a door to their right, which led to the lobby, "but I can hold her for a few minutes."

"Thank you, Chief," Isenguard said, heading to the interrogation room. "I'll move fast."

—m—

The door opened, Inspector Isenguard limping into the room.

Let him talk first. Olivia crossed her legs, not breaking eye contact with him.

The inspector took a seat at the table in front of her, his expression neutral. "Your lawyer's outside."

"Good to know," she said, noting the labored tone in his voice. "I hope your people are okay."

"Thanks for that. Of course, they might've been better if you'd been honest with us about your intentions before requesting our services."

"If you mean my conduct at Bridge Row—"

"I mean that you attended college with the Solomons," Isenguard clarified, tapping the table with his fingers in an annoying rhythm. "And that the three of you were *very* close."

So much for being secretive. Olivia sighed, her calm façade breaking for only a second. "That's true."

"Why didn't you tell us?"

"Because if I did," Olivia answered, "there was a chance you wouldn't let my team see them."

"You mean, we wouldn't let *you* see them," Isenguard said with deadly emphasis, "and you'd be right."

"I'm sorry I lied to—"

"What did you see in their fortress?"

Not even letting me finish my sentence. "The details are foggy, Inspector. Like trying to remember a dream."

"They'd better get clear real damn quick."

"It was alien," Olivia said, noting how Isenguard cracked his knuckles. "Antiseptic and cold. Like a lab or a hospital. The interior was white, like ivory."

"Like the outside," Isenguard said with a touch of impatience. "Give me something else, woman!"

Olivia's brow knotted in thought. "They're not alone."

"What?"

"My theory was correct. The Solomons *did* bring an army with them."

That made Isenguard sit up a little straighter in his seat. "What kind?"

"Helpers," Olivia answered. "They looked like robots."

"And?" Isenguard waved a hand impatiently. "What else?"

"They're how the Solomons altered Gateway City so fast in such a short time." She swallowed before adding, "And they're taking people."

—⁂—

They're taking people. Olivia Blaque's words crystallized Isenguard's worst fear. "You *saw* them take someone?"

"When we were in the control room of their fortress, Stan threw a man at us," she answered distastefully. "One he'd been carrying. It's what stopped us from exploring further."

"Do you know who he was?"

"Stan said his name was Alan Duke."

Jesus, they are *taking people!* Isenguard's throat went dry. "They say *why* they had him?"

"Stan said he was a 'true specimen' of Gateway City."

They're seeing monsters everywhere, because of what happened to their son, Isenguard realized, cold fear gripping his heart, *and they're picking them off like some kind of purge.*

"Do you know what happened to him?"

The disgusted look on Oliva face spoke volumes. "The robots took him. Judging by his screams, I don't think anyone's gonna be seeing him again."

Jesus Christ. The color drained from Isenguard's face. He looked over his shoulder at the mirror, practically hearing Chief Madsen cursing out loud. He leaned close to Olivia as much as the table, and his wounds, would allow. "Did they give you anything else? Anything at all?"

You wanna know what they gave me? Olivia shivered but didn't miss a beat. "Nothing but a lifetime of bad dreams."

"Are you sure?"

"I'm positive, Inspector." It killed her to lie to Isenguard, but she couldn't be sure he would let her leave with the flash drive if he knew she had it. She was sure he suspected Stan had given her something, but he had no way to prove it. Besides, he would learn the truth on an upcoming episode of her show, like everyone else.

"In that case, Mrs. Blaque"—there was a knocking on the door, but Isenguard didn't even turn around— "you're free to go." He cocked his head at the door. "An officer will take your statement before you leave the station."

Olivia got up from the chair and made her way to the door.

"Mrs. Blaque?"

Shit! She stopped, her heard pumping in her chest. "Yes?"

"Try to make us look good," Isenguard answered, not turning to face her. "We got enough bad press as it is."

"I will, Inspector," Olivia answered, managing a sympathetic smile. "I really am sorry about what happened to you and your people."

"I just hope this story of yours was worth it, ma'am. Until next time."

That wasn't bad, she thought as she turned the knob to open the door.

"Oh, and Mrs. Blaque?"

Here it comes.

Olivia stopped just outside of the room. "Yes, Inspector?"

"If you *ever* come to my city and pull what you pulled at Bridge Row again," Isenguard swiveled his head to face her from inside the interrogation room, the gesture downright robotic. "I will nail your hide to my wall."

Nothing aggressive in THAT statement. Olivia swallowed hard, focusing on Isenguard's stone-faced expression. "Understood, Inspector."

"Now get out of here."

—⁂—

"This was supposed to be a covert operation, Isenguard," Madsen muttered, scratching his head. Both men stood in front of a window in Madsen's office, watching Mrs. Blaque walk onto the steps of the station with her lawyer, bathed in the rays of the morning sun.

"And it would've been, if Mrs. Blaque had followed my damn orders," he insisted as they watched Mrs. Blaque and her lawyer step into a waiting car. *We should've kept her here even if we had to falsify some evidence.* "She knows more about the Solomons, Chief. I'm sure of it."

"We can't worry about that now, not with the Solomons doing a purge on our streets!"

I know. Isenguard sighed, a sense of defeat draining his energy. "So what do we do?"

"I have to talk to the mayor about this," Madsen answered, rubbing his hands together as if to warm them. "We may have to call in some … bigger guns."

"Bigger guns?" Isenguard gave Madsen a worried look. "Chief, maybe we should—"

"Go home, Inspector. I'll take it from here."

"But—"

"Now, Inspector."

"Yes, Chief." Isenguard quietly walked away from Madsen's side by the window and left his office.

—⁂—

"Well, I'll be damned, Liv," an excited voice declared the next morning. "You actually pulled it off!"

"Was there any doubt, Terry?"

"Well, a little."

Olivia sat in her hotel room, chatting with her editor, Terry Blight, via Skype. She was still toweling off after a long shower, dressed only in a bathrobe. "I sent the info from the Solomons' flash drive. There anything we can use?"

"Are you kidding?! It's got detailed reports on who they are and their mission statement!" Terry answered in an excited voice. "We even got the footage Richard and Jimmy recorded of them in action! Had me on the edge of my seat!"

"That's a ringing endorsement." Olivia applied a few more eye drops to her eyes.

"Your eyes still bothering you?"

"They've been bothering me since last night. Doctors say I have to add two drops every four hours for the irritation to go away." Olivia's expression grew solemn. "But hey, it could be a hell of a lot worse."

"If you mean Jimmy and Richard, they're gonna be fine," Terry said in a confident voice. "They were on the ground with U.S. troops in the second Iraq War. A few bumps and bruises aren't gonna keep them down."

"They got those bruises following me."

"They knew the risks, Liv. How are *you* doing?"

"I'm fine," Olivia answered, wiping away excess tears from the eyedrops. "Right as rain!"

"Bullshit," Terry stated, a no-nonsense expression on his face. "I know the Solomons were your friends from college. That's why you chose the assignment."

"You know too much about me," Olivia declared, sucking her teeth in annoyance.

"That's what happens when you work with someone who gets chatty when she's had too much wine. Now tell me the truth. Are you all right?"

"It was strange," Olivia admitted reluctantly, "seeing them like that." She paused, letting out a weary sigh. "It was like I was looking at strangers wearing the bodies of my friends."

"Losing a child can do that," Terry said grimly, "even to the best of us."

"What a relief I'll never know that pain."

"You gonna make your flight tomorrow?"

"I'll be fine, Terry," Olivia answered. "Just have that champagne ready when I get back to the office."

"Oh, I will," he answered. "Call me the minute you touch down at the airport."

"I will, Terry. Now get some sleep."

"You too," he said before ending the Skype call.

Olivia sat back in her chair, letting out a tension-filled sigh. She closed her eyes. *Still hurts to blink.*

"Your editor sounds nice."

No. Olivia froze, the voice familiar. *There's no way!*

"You can keep your eyes closed if it helps."

Refusing to be scared, Olivia opened them to see Stan sitting in a chair across from her desk. "Here to execute me?"

"If I wanted you dead, you'd be dead."

He says it so casually.

Olivia licked her lips, fighting the urge to snatch up her phone and call the police. "I thought our business was done."

"It is," Stan answered, a tired expression on his face. "I just wanted to make sure you didn't have any scars from being in our home."

"My eyes aren't bleeding, if that's what you mean."

"I mean psychological scars."

"I'm not banging my head against a wall," Olivia said, trying to keep her tone casual. *At least not yet.* "So on that front, I'm fine."

"That's good to know."

"How'd you get past hotel security?"

"It's funny what you can do when people spend their time looking at their phones and computer screens instead of looking at one another," Stan answered in a smug voice.

"Where's Francine?" Olivia asked, her eyes searching every nook and cranny of her hotel room. *She used to love playing hide-and-seek with us back in college.*

"Resting," Stan answered, watching her with interest in his brown eyes. Or was it regret? "She's been through a lot."

"So did the police officers I was with."

"You put them in our sights, Liv," Stan declared in a calm yet accusatory voice. "You brought them to *our* home."

"Still, what you did to them," Olivia said, shaking her head in disgust, "you could've killed them."

"But we didn't," Stan said, giving her a dispassionate look, "which is more than I can say for what they did to our son."

—w—

You can't keep blaming them for Brian, Olivia thought, giving him a sympathetic look. "Why are you really here, Stan?"

"To make sure you sent the appropriate people our message."

"Did you hear my conversation with my editor?"

"I did," Stan answered, giving her a smooth nod of his head.

You were in my room that long and I didn't see you? There was a time when Olivia didn't need to hear or see Stan to know he was near. *I'm losing my edge.* "You just heard it, Stan. My editor got it."

"But will he publish it?"

"There a reason he wouldn't?" Olivia was on high alert, treating Stan's words as a thinly veiled threat. After the obvious threat she got from Isenguard back at the GCPD station, she was very defensive. Olivia had once thought Stan would never hurt her, but that was before he tossed a screaming, frightened human being to his robot servants as though he were a toy.

"He answers to a boss, same as you," Stan answered, giving her a stern glance. "A lot of bosses, as a matter of fact. Bosses that might silence him if they feel threatened by what we have to say."

Olivia had wondered that herself. Terry was all smiles during their Skype call, but what about when she arrived at the studio a few days later? "I won't let that happen. I'll stake my career on it."

"That won't matter," Stan said as he got up from his seat. "You're only as effective as those higher on the totem pole want you to be."

You've grown so cynical, Olivia thought, watching with longing eyes. *Hurts me so much to see you like this. You and Francine.*

"You're leaving?"

"Yes, I am."

No, no, no, no! Olivia sprang from her seat and ran to Stan, throwing her arms around him. "Stan, please! Stop what you're doing! Before it's too late!"

"Liv, I have to—"

"You don't have to do anything! All you have to do is leave! You and Francine! Just stop whatever you're thinking of doing and leave!" Olivia looked up at him, desperation in her eyes. "Make new lives for yourselves, away from all this! I can help you!" She gave his waist a tight squeeze. "I'll help you!"

"We made a promise, Liv."

"Whatever you promised Brian isn't worth your lives! He'd know that!"

"I wasn't talking about Brian."

—◊◊◊—

"I'll never talk!" Alan Duke thrashed against the surgical chair he found himself strapped to, surrounded by cold, oppressive, gunmetal-gray walls. "You hear me? Never!"

"Oh, you'll talk." Francine stared at him, her gaze dispassionate as she stood a few feet in front of him. "Everyone talks, when you apply the right pressure. I learned that from my time teaching in public school."

The robots hovered above him, surgical tools at the ends of their tendrils. They turned to her, waiting for her word.

She nodded.

"I got friends, bitch!" Alan called out as the robots descended on him. "They'll find me, you hear?! They'll find me!"

81

"And we'll deal with them." Francine floated out of his room, down a long hallway, the walls and floor as gray as Duke's room. Rooms identical to Alan's honeycombed the walls. "We'll deal with *all* of you."

She whistled as Alan's screams echoed down the hall.

IT WAITS IN THE DARK

Officer Kevin Jacobson took a sniper's perch in a dingy motel room on the edge of town, sucking in careful breaths to keep from passing out. Two hands rested on his gun for stability. A stabbing pain in his side hinted at cracked ribs, maybe more.

Stay awake. He blinked his eyes rapidly to keep stars from dancing across his vision. *You need to stay awake!*

Grass and dirt stains speckled his clothes, blood from scores of cuts and bruises running down his legs. Kevin kept his 9mm trained on the door, his hands shaking from exhaustion.

Focus. He took careful breaths to keep from passing out, the inside of his mouth tasting like metal.

Focus, dammit.

Kevin sighted through his gun's scope, finger on the trigger. He centered his crosshairs on the door. *It'll be here soon. Saw it just behind me.* He glanced feverishly at a window to his left. *Is it gonna come through the door? Or the window? Not sure I can cover both! Just gotta give it a target ... so it doesn't go after her or anyone else!*

But he knew so many people, and it knew that.

It had a laundry list of people to get to before him!

For all Kevin knew, it had gotten to his friends and was just saving him for last! *No!* He shook the hellish thought away. He wiped at his red hair, coming away with sweat, grime, and blood.

I can't think that. I can't think—

Things went dark.

No!

His eyes shot open, his head throbbing. *How long was I out? I know I was out!* He checked a clock on the wall. *A minute, maybe two! I've been out for two minutes!*

And it hadn't come. Maybe it never would! Maybe he was spared!

No, it saw him. It had to come for him! He was the last loose end!

God, Kevin thought, wiping at his nose, *is this what it was like for Kate when the Solomons attacked?! Did she even have time to be scared! God, I'd take the Solomons over this thing!*

He was about to consider prayer when the door to his hotel room buckled.

Shit, it's here! It's fucking here! He aimed his gun on the door, waiting for his pursuer to break it down. *C'mon, you son of a bitch! C'mon!*

—◊◊◊—

The Gateway City Police Station was silent as a tomb when Officer Kevin Jacobson arrived a few days earlier, everyone still in shock at what they had found at Kate Barrow's home.

Or, more accurately, what was left of it.

Can't believe they got her, Kevin thought disparagingly. *I knew the Solomons were angry, but to kidnap a cop like that?!* He sat at his desk, speechless. *They know I was her partner. They gonna be looking for me too?*

"Jacobson."

Warily, Kevin looked up, seeing Inspector Isenguard looking at him from Chief Madsen's office. "Yes?"

"Chief needs to see you."

Shit. Kevin's mouth went dry. "I'm on my way."

—◊◊◊—

"How's the arm, Jacobson?" GCPD Commissioner Topher Madsen asked as he shuffled papers from behind his desk.

Starting with small talk, I see. "Still broke, sir," Kevin answered. He glanced at his left arm, which was still resting in a sling, after Stan

Solomon almost broke it the day Kate killed his son. "Should be in working order, in a few days."

"Good to hear, Jacobson," Madsen said dismissively. "Good to hear."

"Uh, when can I go back on duty?"

"Not for a while," Madsen answered, still not looking at him. "Maybe never again."

That mean I'm fired? Jacobson cleared his throat. "Is what I heard about the Solomons true? Are they really superhuman?"

"I wish they weren't, but they are."

"And Detective Drake and Benz?"

"Drake's convalescing in a hospital. Benz is with him."

"How are they?"

"Better than expected," Madsen answered. "Much better, in fact."

"Did the Solomons really blow up Kate Barrow's house? With Benz in it? With lightning from the freaking sky?"

"That they did."

So they're superhumans. "How is Benz still alive?"

"According to her report, Stan and Francine protected her from the brunt of the blast."

How nice of them. "Can I see them?" Kevin asked. "Give 'em my best wishes?"

"You got bigger things to worry about, though God bless you for asking."

Wait, what? Kevin's brow arched in confusion. "Bigger things, sir?"

Madsen took a puff off his cigar. "Do I really have to spell it out for you?"

"Sir?"

"You were Kate's partner. The Solomons took her, and they know you were her partner. Hell, Stan got in a tussle with you the day Kate killed their son."

Dammit, that's true, Kevin thought, letting out a slow, anxious breath. *They gonna come after me, next?* "So, she was kidnapped because of that?"

"She was," Madsen answered, giving the beat cop a regretful, sorrowful look.

"Then ..." Kevin paused, but only for a second, "we have to get her back!"

"I know that, Jacobson," came the strained answer. "We all know that."

Then what are we waiting for?! Kevin thought, giving Madsen a mystified, frantic look. "We have to do this now!"

"We've no idea where Kate is," Madsen said in a blunt, no-nonsense voice. "At least, not yet."

"Then we canvas the damn neighborhoods! All of them!" Kevin found himself shaking with rage at the thought of Kate Barrow, chained up and at the mercy of Stan and Francine Solomon. *Good lord, who knows what they're doing to her while we sit here jabbering!* "We knock down doors! We bust heads! We do what we have to do to get her—!"

"We got folks working on that," Madsen said, cutting him off. "I'm worried about you right now."

Huh? "Why would you—"

"Stan Solomon broke your arm for killing his kid ..."

"Sir, I didn't—"

"You think he won't finish the job?"

—⁂—

"Baby?" Joan Collins, Kevin's girlfriend, said as they sat at the dinner table in his home, a few hours after his talk with Madsen. "It's not your fault." She put a supportive hand on his shoulder, as he stared solemnly at the ham and eggs she'd prepared for him. "You know that, right?"

"I know, babe," Kevin said as he picked at his food. "It's just ... it feels like it is."

"I know."

"I should've done more."

"Kate took the shot."

"And I should've stopped her," Kevin declared, almost launching out of his seat. "Chased after her! Called her back! Something! If I'd done my freaking job, that Solomon kid would still be alive!" *And Kate would still be here, not held against her will with those freaks!* The thought of her, being the Solomons plaything, gave him the shakes all over again!

"Honey," Joan said, in a soothing voice as she massaged a tense knot in the back of Kevin's neck, "Kate was always gung-ho, you know that."

"But I was the senior," Kevin insisted. "I was supposed to watch her back."

"You did," Joan said, pointing at his arm in the sling. *"And* got that."

"This is *all* I got. Kate lost her livelihood, maybe her life. Doesn't seem fair."

"I don't know all about that."

Kevin drearily stared out the window, taking in the nighttime sky. "And now she's with them. Alone."

"What about Drake and Benz?"

"The hospital's keeping him for observation. Benz is on convalescence leave."

Joan arched an eyebrow. "But they'll be okay. Right ..." The words trailed off as she spoke.

"Yeah," Kevin said, his expression brightening a little. "They'll be okay."

"Thank heaven for that."

Yeah. "But Kate won't be."

—៣—

"Yes, sir," Kevin said, holding his phone to his ear in the kitchen. "I understand."

"Who was that?" Joan asked from the living room.

"Chief Madsen." Kevin hung up the phone. "He's putting me on paid leave."

"Well, *that's* good news."

I wish it was, Kevin thought glumly. *But that's how it started with Kate.*

—៣—

87

Later at home by himself, Kevin was watching a football game when he heard a knock at his door. Sighing, he got to his feet. He grabbed his gun—in case the visitor was nuts—and approached the door as the knocking continued. *Who could want to talk at this hour?* Kevin peered through the peephole. *Oh.*

Letting out a deep breath, he opened the door. "Hello, Ms. Barrow." He recognized her from a photo in Kate's phone.

"Officer Jacobson." The woman's gaze was firm, her eyes piercing. She looked like Kate, but her hair was shorter. And red, instead of black. And fashioned into a pixie cut, the sides cut close to her skin.

She was dressed in black. Either she was in mourning or just liked the color.

She looked damned good in black.

"How can I help you?"

"Am I catching you at a bad time?"

"No," Kevin answered, noting he was wearing sweatpants. "Come in."

Ms. Barrow did just that. "I don't see you at the station."

"They put me on leave."

"That's how it started with Kate."

"I know," Kevin said, throwing on a T-shirt. "Can I get you anything?"

"Tea, if you have it."

"Right," he said, putting a kettle full of water on the stove. "One cup of tea, coming up."

"So how are you holding up?"

How am I holding up? How are you holding up?!

"Fair to middling." There was no way to talk to Ms. Barrow without addressing Kate's kidnapping. He hated being in a situation like this, but here he was.

"I wish I could say the same," she said as she took the cup Kevin handed her. "But I get by."

"Still no word?"

"I don't think the department's looking for her anymore."

"I wouldn't say that …"

"It's been weeks, Officer …"

"Just call me Kevin."

"Kevin," Ms. Barrow said, as if trying out the feel. "It's been weeks."

"That's true," Kevin admitted, trying to show sympathy.

"That's why I'm here. I need you to find Kate. I need you to find my daughter."

—⁂—

"Ms. Barrow, I have no authority to conduct an investigation."

"You're the only person I can turn to!"

"I don't even know where to start looking."

"But I do," Ms. Barrow said confidently. "I even know who to speak to."

Oh no, Kevin thought darkly. "If you mean Detective Drake, I gotta tell you—"

"He was there when they took her!"

"Getting his ass handed to him trying to defend her."

"And now he's conveniently in the hospital," she spat. "Under *their* lock and key."

"He's being treated for injuries, Ms. Barrow. He can't answer *any* questions."

"You don't know that."

"You don't either," Kevin shot back. "You've not been there."

"Actually ...," Ms. Barrow said.

Crap. Kevin rubbed his eyes, suddenly feeling very tired. "When did this happen?"

"After he was brought in. They said he was in a coma, but I know they're protecting him."

"Who's 'they'? The doctors? They're doing their jobs, Ms. Barrow."

"They're hiding something," she said. "I brought it up to Madsen, and he didn't give me a straight answer."

"He's dealing with a lot," Kevin said. *We all are.*

"He's *not* dealing with a missing daughter."

Mrs. Tunnel Vision over here. "And you want me to do your dirty work."

"I *want* you to find my daughter."

89

Dammit to hell. "I'll see what I can do," Kevin promised reluctantly.

—⁂—

I can't *believe I'm doing this,* Kevin thought as he walked through the halls of Madison General, the hospital Drake had been taken to. The place smelled of death and dying, one of the reasons he hated hospitals.

The second he stepped through the doors, he wanted to gag. He put it up to jitters. *Yeah, I'm just investigating a case that no one wants to touch because of a grieving mother. Why would I have any jitters?*

Kevin walked to an elevator, mindful of the curious looks he got. While his face had been in the papers during Kate's trial, the focus had been on her. Because of that, only some of the public recognized him when he was out in town.

Yet, they didn't seem to hate him as much as they did her.

Kevin patted the Taser in his jacket pocket and stepped into the elevator. The Taser wasn't as good as his gun, but it was the only thing he was sure he could get into the hospital without incident.

In case he had to defend himself.

He clenched and unclenched his fists as he remembered the floor Ms. Barrow said Drake's room was on.

The doors opened at the fifth floor, and he stepped out. His eyes flicked to one side of the hall, then to the other.

Room 585. That's the room he's staying in.

It was a few minutes before he found it.

—⁂—

"I can't believe I'm doing this," a nurse said as she met Kevin outside Drake's room.

"Relax, Jackie, I'm only going to talk to him."

"But you're not supposed to be here," she whispered as she checked the hall behind him. "No one is! He needs to get his rest!"

"Then I should get in there quick," Kevin said. "Before someone's tipped off about my visit."

"If you weren't holding my habit over my head—"

"Well, I am, so let's get this done."

"You're a bastard," the nurse declared, giving him an icy look, "you know that?"

"And I'm crying about it," Kevin said sarcastically. "Now how much time do I have?"

"Ten minutes," she spat after a few seconds of fuming silence. "Maybe less."

"Then I'd better get in there. Keep a look out. Signal me when guards come back."

"Right," the nurse said, scratching at her exposed arms. "Well, in you go."

Yeah, in I go, Kevin thought as he stepped into Drake's room. *Ready or not.*

—๗—

Detective Frank Drake was in a bed in the center of the room. The mayor had sprung for it, putting up his own funds to pay for it and ensure his privacy.

Jackie's right, Kevin thought as he approached Drake's bed. *I shouldn't be here.*

Drake's neck was in a brace, the right side of his face swollen under a mess of bandages. The rest of his body was under a blanket. The way he fidgeted hinted at other wounds just under the covers.

"Wondered when you'd come by," he rasped, fixing his good eye on Kevin.

"Heard me come in, eh?"

"Nurse Jackie gave me a heads-up a few minutes ago," Drake answered, his unbandaged eye staring at him. "How do you know her?"

"We go way back," Kevin answered. "We came up together."

"Uh-huh," Drake grunted dismissively. "Let me guess. Kate's mom put you up to this."

"You guessed it."

"She thinks I know where her daughter is."

"She does?"

Drake rolled his eye, letting out a pained sigh. "So what do you want from me?"

"I know you told everyone what you could, but I find that given time, new thoughts arrive," Kevin answered while looking over his shoulder at the entrance to the hall. "Profound ideas that can make or break a case."

"Well," Drake admitted. "I *have* been thinking about that night."

"Figured you would be."

"Been all I've been thinking about, actually."

"Think of me as a sounding board," Kevin said good-naturedly.

"A sounding board that's off the force," Drake declared, his good eye swiveling back toward Kevin. "Grasping at straws."

"Easy, Drake," Kevin said, raising his hands. "I'm just on leave. Paid leave, in fact."

"Wasn't that how it started with Kate?"

"I'm not her," Kevin insisted, tapping his chest so hard, he was sure his fingers left bruises. *No WAY I'm going down like she did!*

"Heh, not yet."

"C'mon Drake, tell me something," Kevin said, looking over his shoulder at the door behind him, again. "We don't have long here."

"I'll help you as best I can," Drake said after letting a grunt of pain. "But I gotta know one thing, first."

"Anything, man. Anything."

"Why didn't you stop Kate from killing Brian Solomon?"

—m—

"If I tell you," Kevin said, shifting uncomfortably in his seat, "will you tell me what you know?"

"Yes," Drake answered.

"And it doesn't leave this room?"

"You see a wire anywhere?"

Strange answer.

Kevin got up from his chair to search the room, in case Madsen had it bugged. He heard a rumor, through the office grapevine, that he had served Kate up on a platter and she had been the pride of the department. If Madsen could do that to her, he would ditch Kevin in a minute.

"The room's not bugged, Jacobson."

"I know," Kevin said, returning to his seat by Drake's bedside.

"And yet you searched for one," the injured detective added.

And boy, do I feel stupid for that. "Had to be sure."

"That distrust," Drake sighed, trying to shake his head and failing. "That's gonna kill us, way before the Solomons do."

"You a philosopher now?"

"Got nothing else to do here. Now tell me, why'd you let Kate kill that boy?"

—⁕—

"I didn't let her do anything," Kevin insisted as he scooted his chair closer to Drake's bedside. "I merely let her apprehend a fleeing suspect." *And I just contradicted myself.*

"On her own."

"She's faster than me."

"You were the primary," Drake shot back. "You shouldn't have let her chase a suspect alone, without backup."

"I called it in! And arrived on the scene!"

"After Brian Solomon had been killed. What took you so long?"

"Securing a rowdy suspect," Kevin answered, looking away. "Look, Drake, I didn't know things were gonna get that bad."

"Nice way to apologize."

"That Solomon kid should've stayed indoors!"

"Kate should've given him and his family fair warning before turning their front yard into a shooting gallery."

"I know that!" Kevin hissed. "I didn't think things were gonna escalate the way they did! I told her to wait for me! But you know how gung-ho she was!" Kevin winced, realizing he had referred to her in the past tense.

Mrs. Barrow wasn't going to like that.

"Just like you," Drake said.

Kevin's brow arched angrily. "Excuse me?"

—⟊—

"Don't get indignant with me," Drake warned, raising a shaky finger to his face. "You shared a car with Kate for months. You're telling me you didn't teach her any bad habits?"

"I'm a good cop," Kevin said defensively.

"We're all good cops," Drake said, licking scarred lips. "But we're not perfect."

"We're not monsters, either." *No matter what anyone says.*

"Really? I've heard things …"

Here we go. Kevin sucked his teeth. "Those police brutality charges were dropped!"

"Your accusers changed their story." Drake hesitated before adding, "After you paid them a 'visit.'"

"You said you wouldn't judge me," Kevin said, shrinking from Drake's words.

"You feeling judged, Jacobson?"

Enough of this bullshit! "I told you my story," Kevin said, banging a fist against the railing of Drake's hospital bed. "Now tell me what you know!"

"I know Brian Solomon was sixteen," Drake said, wincing in pain from a host of unseen injuries. "Not even a man yet."

"I know that!"

"And now he never will be."

"You think that doesn't bother me?!" Kevin hissed through clenched teeth. He was sure he could practically feel beads of sweat running down his forehead. "That I don't think about that every day?!"

"And now, thanks to the two of you, every cop in Gateway City's got a target on their back," Drake continued. "You think doing Ms. Barrow's dirty work's gonna wash that off?"

Kevin gripped his shoulders in quiet desperation. "Tell! Me! Something!"

"Best place for answers, I figure, is the Solomons' home."

"A team of investigators have already *been* there! They found nothing!"

"You sure about that?"

This isn't a joke you son of a-! Kevin felt his phone vibrate in his pocket, a signal that Drake's guards were on the way back. *Dammit!* "You better hope you're right, Drake," he declared as he headed for the door. "Or I'll be seeing you again!"

"I'll be here," Drake shot back as Kevin left the hospital room.

—⟋⟍—

All items taken from the Solomons' house are at the station, Kevin thought as he got to his car in the hospital parking lot. *And there's no way Madsen's gonna let me take a peek.*

There had to be another way.

I can't let it end here, Kevin thought as he slipped into the driver's seat. He gripped the steering wheel in frustration. *I owe Kate too much!*

He felt his phone vibrate. Looking at the screen, he saw it was Nurse Jackie.

You find what you needed? her text read.

It's a start. Guards suspect anything?

No. A pause. *Will Drake talk?*

No, Kevin texted back. He didn't swear him to secrecy, but he knew Drake wouldn't say anything. *Your secret is safe. Just stay out of trouble.*

Then the phone rang.

It was Ms. Barrow.

Is she watching me?

Kevin put the phone to his ear, taking quick glances at the parking lot around his car. "Hello, Ms. Barrow."

"Did you learn anything?"

"Got one lead. The Solomons' house."

"The police were already there."

"They might've missed something," Kevin said. "I'll head there in the morning."

"I'll meet you at your place," Ms. Barrow said. "We need to trade notes."

Of course we do, he thought sarcastically.

—⟋⟍—

Kevin returned to his apartment, dreading another conversation with Kate's mom. *How long do I have before she gets here? Maybe forty minutes?*

The minute she left his home last night, Kevin got on the computer and found out exactly how far her home was from his.

He also discovered that she and her husband were estranged.

Losing a child could do that.

After his sister, Marla, died from cancer, Kevin's parents couldn't stand being around each other. As though seeing each other – and him – was a constant reminder of their failure.

So Kate's mom moved out of their home, purchasing a studio near Kate's neighborhood.

She had gotten more than a few restraining orders from those neighbors, who just wanted to be left alone. Kevin had no clue how they got restraining orders against someone simply asking questions, but there it was.

He glanced at the door, hoping Joan would walk in. *Maybe she needs a little incentive.* He looked up her number on his phone and gave her a call.

"Hey, babe, wanna do something tonight?" *Please say yes!*

"Turn from this path."

"You're not Joan." Kevin stiffened, his face growing as white as a sheet. "Who is this?"

"Kate Barrow walked a cursed road," the raspy voice growled. "One that led to a bloody end."

Kevin's blood froze. "Who are you?"

"Her end need not be yours."

"Who the hell is this?!" Kevin ran to the window, his eyes searching the street outside his home. "Do you work for the Solomons?! Tell me!"

"But it can be," the voice said as he spied a large shape on the roof of the building across from his. "It *can* be."

He's gotta be close! Kevin broke through the door of his home, too hyped up to use a key. *I can get to him!* He blew past an astonished Ms. Barrow. "No time to talk!"

He went down the steps, hitting the street in record time.

Where?!

He looked up and saw the figure.

There you are!

It had ivory-colored scales and pointed ears that looked like horns.

Good lord ...

Kevin's mouth hung open.

Mrs. Barrow was beside him, watching the same thing he was, completely speechless.

The figure threw something at Kevin's feet and then vaulted into the sky on leathery wings.

"I never knew," Mrs. Barrow gasped, eyes bulging with shock. "Never dreamed!"

"You and me both," Kevin agreed, trying to recover his thoughts.

"Does that thing has my daughter?!"

"We don't know yet." *Why would she make that connection? She just saw the thing, same time as I did!*

Then it hit Kevin. The Solomons weren't human anymore, Ms. Barrow had to have known that. The thing on the roof wasn't human either. It was a flimsy connection, but it was enough to have her freaking out.

"What are the Solomons involved in?! Did they conjure that thing?!"

"Mrs. Barrow!" Kevin barked, shaking her roughly by the shoulders. "Calm down!"

"I ..." She blinked. One time. Then two. "Okay, I'm all right."

"Are you sure?"

"Yes, I'm sure! Now let go of me!"

"Okay, then." Kevin went to grab whatever the thing had tossed at him, then stopped cold.

It was Joan's cell phone; he recognized the Mickey Mouse sticker on the back. She was a huge Disney fan. Had been since she was little girl.

She'd never part with her phone willingly. Never let it leave her purse or pocket. Sweat beaded on Kevin's face. *It knows about her. It knows how to find her!*

What it if broke into her home, attacked her to send him a message?! What if it was roughing her up while he stood around with his dick in hands?!

Kevin ran for his car, jumped in, and sped off for Joan's home.

—m—

Five minutes of hectic driving later, Kevin ran up the stairs leading to Joan's apartment. He blew past every traffic light and stop sign on the way.

Stupid, stupid, stupid! The Solomons got a mad-on for us, why wouldn't they send someone after the people we love?!

He didn't bother calling for backup. If that thing was already in Joan's home, he wanted it to himself.

And if it hurt a hair on her head …

"Joan?!" Kevin arrived at her door, panting viciously. "You in there?! Open up, please!" He banged on her door furiously, visions of her in that thing's clutches playing havoc with his mind. "Goddammit, girl! Open up!"

When he got no answer, Kevin whipped out his gun and fired, shattering the lock. *Sorry, baby!* He kicked the door open and dashed inside. *I'll pay for a new one!*

Darkness greeted him.

Looking around frantically, he called out for Joan again.

No answer.

Where is she?! Kevin thought as he searched the living room, bedroom, kitchen, and bathroom. *Where the hell is she?!*

He heard the murmurs of neighbors in the hall.

Oh! This *wakes the neighbors! Not the noise of a demon possibly breaking into their apartment! No,* my *noise wakes them up! Bunch of incompetent, sons of—*

Feeling someone approaching him from behind, Kevin turned quickly to face them.

———⟊———

A surprised Joan stared at him, grocery bags in her hands.

"Thank God you're alive!" Kevin said, giving her a grateful hug.

"Of course I'm alive," she answered, sounding a little frightened. "Something happening there, hon?"

"Where have you been?!"

"I had to work late tonight. I told you that yesterday."

Did she? It was hard for Kevin to be sure. The days had started bleeding together since Kate's kidnapping.

"Did you knock down my door?!" Joan gawked at the path of destruction that Kevin made getting into her home. "Why the hell'd you do that?!"

"I was looking for you!"

"You wanna find me, call me on my phone!"

"You mean," Kevin fished her phone out of his pocket, "this phone?!"

"I—" Joan did a double take. "How'd you get my—" she checked her purse, coming up empty. "I just had it—"

It took her phone while she was working, Kevin realized, feeling sick. *It was in the same building she was, and she didn't see it!*

How good was this thing at hiding?!

———⟊———

"Hey there, partner."

The calm, collected voice made Kevin and Joan turn to the busted door.

Standing there, with uniforms behind him, was Inspector Isenguard.

Crap, Kevin cursed mentally. "Uh, hey."

"Got some noise complaints," the giant said as he strode inside Joan's apartment. He glanced at the door. "This you?"

"Uh, yeah," Kevin said, a tremor of shame passing over his face. "It's me."

"Right. Gonna need an explanation on that."

"I wouldn't mind having one either," Joan added heatedly.

Kevin realized how bad it looked. Covered in sweat, eyes wide—he looked like a freaking maniac. He had to give an explanation.

But could he be sure Isenguard, Joan, or Chief Madsen would believe him?

"Waiting for that answer," Isenguard stated patiently.

Shooting Joan an apologetic glance, Kevin approached him. "I'll tell you at the station."

"Yeah, why don't we head on down there for a spell?"

Kevin didn't fight as he felt Isenguard's large hand clamp on his shoulder, leading him out of Joan's apartment.

Least I'm not in handcuffs, Kevin thought as he sat in interrogation at the GCPD ten minutes later. He looked up as Madsen and Isenguard entered the room. "Chief, let me explain—"

"Take a breath," Madsen interrupted as he closed the door. He tossed Kevin a bottle of water. "From what Isenguard told me, you had one hell of a scare."

He's not mad, Kevin thought as he took a gulp of water. *Why isn't he mad?*

He noticed Isenguard leaning against the wall near the entrance to the room, keeping his eyes on him. *No suspicion there.*

"Is Joan okay?"

"She's fine," Madsen answered. "I got the best people with her."

Same thing he said to Kate, Kevin thought as he took another gulp of water.

"So," Madsen said after a few minutes of patient looks. "Why don't you tell me what you're doing working with Mrs. Barrow?"

Damn. Kevin winced, his lips becoming a firm line on his face. "So you know about that."

"There are a lot of things I know, Jacobson."

Except how to protect your people, Kevin thought, giving Madsen a resentful look. "She wants me to find her daughter."

"And how's *that* going?"

"I got a lead," Kevin answered, "on someone I believe is working for the Solomons."

That made Madsen and Isenguard stiffen. "Would this individual happen to be as ... gifted as the Solomons?"

"Yes. And I believe he's stalking me."

"What evidence do you have?"

"He called me using Joan's phone. Suggested I not look into Kate's abduction. That's why I was at Joan's place. I wanted to make sure he wasn't with her, hurting her to send me a message." Kevin looked down at the table, embarrassed. "I didn't mean to scare her."

"Well you did," Isenguard stated in an annoyed voice.

"I know."

Madsen sighed, scratching his head. "Did anyone else see this individual besides you?"

"It's not a person," Kevin insisted. "It's something else."

"Something else?"

"Something not human."

"How do you know that?"

"It had wings!" Kevin shouted, almost shooting up from his chair as though he was hit with 1,000 volts of electricity. "And it flew from the building across from me! From its roof! Probably had claws too! Call Mrs. Barrow in here! She'll say the same thing! She saw it the same time I did!"

"Right. About that," Madsen muttered. "Why didn't you tell us what you were doing with her?"

"I thought I would be giving a grieving mother some closure," Kevin answered truthfully. "I had *no* idea it would blow up into this."

"Grieving mother," Madsen chuckled humorlessly. "Barrow's been using that bit for weeks now ..."

"Chief, I—"

"And you're the *only* rube that fell for it."

And here's the judgment, Kevin thought, realizing that on some level, Madsen was right. "I'm working with Barrow because no one else is listening to her."

Madsen stared spitefully at the one-way mirror across from the table he and Kevin were sitting at. "How's *that* going for you?"

"Excuse me?"

"How's listening to her going for you?"

"All due respect, Chief," Kevin said, giving him a mystified look, "is that *really* the right question to ask?" *I just told you we have a* monster *in the city!*

"It is right now," Madsen answered as he walked to the mirror. "Son, the department's facing a firing squad. Do you know that?"

Monster, guys! A freaking monster is running loose in this city! "I know we're facing blowback from upstairs, but—"

"The Solomons' activities are painting us in a bad light."

"I think we're doing that ourselves."

"And Ms. Barrow's actions are not helping."

"She's just worried for her daughter."

"She's raising a ruckus, is what she's doing!" Madsen declared vehemently. "And putting a bigger target on our backs!" He gnashed his teeth in impotent rage. "Damn media, the people of this town, they're listening to her nonsense."

"Making us look bad," Isenguard added quietly.

"That's not her intention," Kevin said, trying to get a word in. "She just wants to find Kate. We all do, don't we?"

"Of course we do, but there are ways to do it!"

"What's that supposed to mean?" Kevin asked, getting angry. "There's protecting the innocent and putting away the guilty. There's only *one* way to do that."

"That what got you to sit back when Brian Solomon was being blown away?"

Always coming back to that! "You've been talking to Drake?"

"No," Madsen said, sporting a disappointed expression on his face. "But I know you have."

Goddammit Drake, Kevin thought, cursing to himself. "Drake called you."

"No, his nurse did."

Dammit, Jackie! Kevin balled his hands into fists, visualizing using those fists to break Jackie's face. *We're gonna have ourselves a talk when I get out of this, bitch.*

"I'd let those fists go, if I were you," Isenguard advised him. The giant detective had pushed off from the wall he had been leaning against to stand to his full height.

"Why's that, Isenguard?" Kevin asked, taunting the big man. "Am I scaring you?"

"You really want to see me scared, little man?"

"I think if I can face down a monster, I can take care of you, big man."

"Enough," Madsen said, raising a hand for the growing argument to end. "Stay on task, Isenguard." He looked to Kevin. "Yes, Jacobson, we did have a talk with Drake. And a nurse named Jackie too."

"And she told us quite a tale," Isenguard added, going back to leaning against the wall of the interrogation room, his arms folded. "About extortion."

"Of course she did," Kevin spat. *How about that? An addict, unable to keep a secret!*

"Threatening a nurse? That's pretty low, Jacobson."

"I tell you that a monster threatened me using my girl's phone and you focus on what I did to a nurse?" Kevin asked, his mouth agape in mystified shock. "Listen, it told me Kate met a bloody end! That I would too! That has to mean I'm close to finding her! Doesn't that mean anything to you?!"

"Do you have *any* proof of this"—Madsen sighed, rubbing the bridge of his nose—"monster?"

"Is my word not good enough?"

"Considering who you're trucking with ..."

"Oh, for Christ's sake!"

"Watch your tone, Jacobson," Madsen snapped, giving him a withering glare. "And your step. Or your leave's gonna be a *lot* more permanent." He pointed to the door. "Now get the hell out of my office."

"Yes, sir!" Kevin said, giving the police chief a mock salute.

"Isenguard"—Madsen looked to the giant detective—"make sure he gets home."

"Yes, sir," he said, standing at full attention.

"And *only* home!"

—ɷ—

"Didn't listen to me," Kevin mumbled as he rode in Isenguard's car. "Fucker didn't listen to a word I said!"

"Please don't speak of our chief that way."

"Stop slobbing his knob, Isenguard," Kevin shot back. "We're in a damn crisis, and he's worried about fucking public opinion!"

"He's trying to keep us afloat, Kevin," Isenguard said with a hint of edge to his voice. "And your cowboy routine's not helping."

"Helping? We should be working to get Kate back, not worried about what a few assholes think!"

"Gonna be hard to do that if there's no police department, don't you think?"

That got a surprised look from Kevin. "Excuse me?"

"You really love living on that island of yours," Isenguard said. "While you've been enjoying your *paid* leave, we've been dealing with a firestorm. Don't you watch TV?"

"Like I'm gonna tune in to the dog-and-pony show."

"You might want to, because people are circling the wagons," Isenguard declared as he coasted the police car to a stop at a light. "The mayor? The DA? They're talking about making Madsen resign."

"From the force?"

"No, from the planet. Yes, from the force! There's talk of purges, man! Of our way of life coming to an end!"

No way. "Can they … do that?"

"Yeah, they can," Isenguard said as he came up on Kevin's home. "They've been fixing to for years now, and Kate's mess with the Solomons was the final push."

"But …" Kevin stared at him, his mind struggling for the right thing to say, "it's not her fault!"

"You know that. I know that, but the rest of them? They got a duty to the public."

"What about their duty to us?!"

"That ended the minute—the *second*—you let Kate shoot Brian Solomon dead in a public place, on his family's doorstep!"

Kevin tried not to shrink from Isenguard's glare, but it was like enduring the look of a disappointed dad.

"What happened out there?" Isenguard demanded. "You're smarter than that! Hell, *she* was supposed to be smarter than that!"

"I don't know, okay?" Kevin answered with a hint of irritation. "I don't know."

"You don't know? Is that all you have to say?"

"It's all I got," Kevin answered sorrowfully. "I'm sorry, okay? You gotta believe that."

"Well, that's just peachy," Isenguard muttered as he brought his car to a stop. "You and Kate put a target on *all* our heads, and you're sorry."

"I am," Kevin mumbled, a wave of shame washing over him. "You *have* to believe that."

"All I *believe* is that it doesn't matter how sorry you are," Isenguard said as he gestured for him to leave his car. "We're all paying for it."

—⚈—

Well, that *was terrible*, Kevin thought as he trudged to his apartment. *Madsen's against me. Isenguard's done with me. So's the department.* He stepped through the door to his home, surprised to find it open. *Would've thought someone would've closed it. Unless ...* "Hello, Mrs. Barrow."

"Kevin," the older woman began, running to him. "I'm glad you're all right."

"Define 'all right,'" he said as he felt her arms around him. He cocked an eye at the door, hoping Joan wasn't about to come in. Last thing he needed was *that* drama.

Mrs. Barrow guided him to a sofa. "You were at the station a long time."

"Yes, I was," Kevin agreed. "Getting raked over the coals, in fact."

"And let me guess, delicately urged *not* to work with me."

"It wasn't that delicate."

"Jesus," she swore under her breath. "I'm sorry for putting you through this."

"Nothing for you to apologize for."

"If you want out," Mrs. Barrow said in a tense voice, "I'd understand. I wouldn't ... like it." She had a hard time getting the words out, as if her fear was making it impossible to talk. "But I'd ... understand!"

"No doing," Kevin declared, shaking his head dismissively. "Kate was my partner, and this thing's after me too."

"You have people that depend on you ..."

"And I owe to them to close this case," he said, walking to his bedroom to change clothes. "It's my job to bring monsters to justice, and this thing certainly counts." *Especially if it's working for the Solomons.*

"What makes you think you can stop it?" Mrs. Barrow asked, following behind him. "We don't even know how to find it. Hell, we don't even know if it's working for the Solomons!"

"Yeah." Kevin turned to face her, sorrow in his eyes. "We do."

"How?"

"Mrs. Barrow, it mentioned Kate's name."

She put a hand on her chest, the air seemingly being sucked out of her lungs. "What?"

"When that thing called me, using my girl's phone, it mentioned Kate's name," Kevin repeated grimly. "It said she met a violent end, after the Solomons took her."

Mrs. Barrow's face changed slowly, like milk curdling in the sun. Her eyes went from narrow slits to wide dinner plates. Her jaw quivered, then slowly dropped as she digested Kevin's statement.

She swayed on her feet, almost falling before he caught her. "It knows," she whispered, so quietly he had to lean in close to hear her. "It knows her. It knows my daughter, just like the Solomons!"

Dammit. Really wish I hadn't told you. Kevin bit back a litany of curse words that threatened to erupt from his lips. *Do the Solomons know this is happening? Do they know what this is doing to Kate's family? Her friends? Are they getting off on this?!*

"How are we gonna get her back?" Mrs. Barrow whispered. "How can we even—"

"By finding that thing," Kevin cut in, refusing to let her give in to despair. If she did that, the Solomons would win.

"I know that! But how do we even know where to look?"

"We won't have to."

"Excuse me?"

She's more rattled than I thought. "I was Kate's partner, her senior, and it knows that." He gently set her on a nearby chair, taking her hands in his to calm her nerves. "That's why it's watching me, maybe under the Solomons' orders. Means I don't gotta go after it. I just gotta get it to come after me."

"And how are you going to do that?"

"By going to the Solomons' house."

—◊—

Right then, Joan walked in.

"Honey we have to t—" She locked eyes with Ms. Barrow. "Uh, hi!"

"Hey there, honey," Kevin answered good-naturedly. "You know Ms. Barrow, remember? Kate's mother?"

"Of course." Joan went to her, taking her hands in hers. "I'm his lady. I am so sorry for your loss."

"Thank you," Ms. Barrow said hesitantly. "He's helping me … with counseling."

"Of course." Joan turned to Kevin. "Honey, I'll be in the den, doing some … light reading."

"Right," he said, recognizing the phrase they had used when they felt tense. "Just gonna see her off."

"Right then," Joan said, leaving the living room. "If you need anything, Ms. Barrow, let me know."

"I sure will," she said, giving Joan a wave she didn't return. She turned to Kevin. "I should be on my way."

"Might be a good idea," he said, his muscles tensing for a fight he knew was coming.

"Did I … cause something?"

"What? No. She's a sweetheart." It would take more than seeing a woman in his house to make Joan question their relationship.

And Ms. Barrow wasn't a stranger.

"I'll see you tomorrow, then," she said, making her way to the door. "Don't do anything without me."

"No problem," Kevin said as he showed her out. "The minute I make a move, you'll be the first to know." He gave her a steady smile before shutting the door.

—⁕—

"So," Joan started as Kevin turned to face her. "What's this I'm hearing about you working a case for Kate's mom?"

"I was gonna tell you." *Eventually.*

"Would this case happen to be about Kate's kidnapping?"

"It would," Kevin answered. *Just get to the argument.*

"And *that* got you to break into my apartment?"

"I didn't break in, per se—"

"Kevin," Joan said, giving him a scathing glare.

"Yeah, it is," he admitted. He never could last long under her glare. "Whatever took Kate was spying on you, so—"

"The Solomons took Kate."

I know that! "But this creature's working *for* them."

Joan scratched her forehead, an exasperated look on her face. "A creature."

"Yes." Kevin knew how crazy it sounded. *This is why I don't tell you things!*

"Is working for the Solomons," she continued, looking as if she were struggling to understand what was going on.

"Yes." *And this is making it worse!*

"And this creature," Joan finished, her brow arched in disbelief, "had my phone."

"Yeah," Kevin said, feeling the ice cracking around him. *Just believe me!*

"And it … what?" She looked at him, gesturing expectantly. "Tried to call you with it?"

"Yeah," he answered, growing angry that it was taking his girlfriend *this* long to catch up, "to warn me off the case."

"Right," Joan said, looking away for a second. She turned to face him again. "Baby, I love you …"

"I know."

"But that's the craziest thing I've ever heard."

"I know," Kevin agreed, shaking his head. *You have no idea.* "But it's the truth. It's the world we live in now."

"Why? Because the Solomons are superhumans now?"

"Yeah," he said, looking at her with barely concealed impatience. "I *told* you that!"

"Honey, Kate was kidnapped," Joan said with forced patience. "And that's terrible, but that doesn't mean the Solomons have superpowers."

"I told you what happened …"

"Which you got from someone else. You didn't see it with your own eyes, did you?"

"No, but I saw that thing with my own eyes," Kevin protested. "And so did Ms. Barrow."

Joan cocked an eyebrow. "The one that put you on this case?"

"Yes!" Kevin practically shouted. "Why is this so hard for you?"

"Oh I don't know, because I'm still getting over finding my boyfriend breaking into my apartment like a crazy man!"

"I told you why I did that!"

"And then seeing him get hauled away like a freaking criminal!"

"Isenguard did that to please your neighbors."

"Who called him because you broke into my apartment!" Joan shouted. "After, by the way, you shot my lock off with your gun, in a public place, without warning!"

Son of a … Kevin had to walk away before he did something he would regret. *Ever since that Solomon kid got shot, our word's meant mud! Does decades of keeping these assholes safe mean nothing!?* Once he composed himself, he spoke calmly. "I'm sorry my behavior scared you—"

"That's an understatement."

"But I was trying to keep you safe," he finished. "Whether you believe me or not, this thing knows where you live and can get to you anytime it wants."

"I'll … concede that," Joan said reluctantly.

"You're on its radar."

"Because you're working with Ms. Barrow."

"I *know* that. But you've got to realize you're in danger."

"And what am I supposed to do?"

"Oh, I don't know, run, for Pete's sake?" Kevin answered desperately. "Leave the city? Go to your folks in Jersey?"

"So I can endanger them too?" Joan threw her hands up in disbelief. "I don't think so."

"It won't come after you," Kevin insisted, grabbing her shoulders. "It's only after me."

"You *just* said I'm on its radar."

"And you are, but it won't bother you. It'll be too focused on me."

"Why would it ..." Then the realization dawned on Joan's face. "You're gonna continue this case, aren't you?"

"I owe it to Kate and her mother."

"For God's sake, Kevin," Joan said in a strained voice, "doing this won't bring Kate back!"

"You don't know that."

"Kevin, Stan and Francine's pain runs deep. They're not gonna give Kate back until they *want* to give her back."

"Like I said ... *you don't know that!*"

"Yelling at me like I'm some damn kid's not gonna get me to see your point." Joan's eyes flashed with anger as she took a menacing step toward him.

"Whether it does or not," Kevin said, his eyes narrowing to slits, "I'm gonna follow this case, wherever this leads. You can either get on board or get out of my way."

"Oh, *are* you?" Joan's jaw clenched as her fiery glare bore into his skull. "Well, since you're so *committed* to this ..."

Oh shit! "Now hold on," Kevin said, taking a step back from her as though she was an erupting volcano. "Let me recraft my response ..."

"You can do it without me!" She grabbed her jacket and stormed out of his apartment. She slammed the door as she left, causing a few pictures to fall to the floor.

"Shit," Kevin cursed under his breath.

—ɯ—

A chilly wind whipped through the Solomons' neighborhood, making Kevin stuff his hands in his coat pockets. *Maybe I should've brought backup. Or at least worn warmer clothes!*

What if the Solomons' pet monster was nearby, waiting to snatch him up?

Maybe it was one of their supporters. He saw so many at Kate's trial.

So many eyes.

Piercing, accusing eyes.

Kevin felt Francine Solomon's eyes boring into his skull like lasers. Stan was behind her, his hands on her shoulders. Meant to keep her from jumping over the courtroom fence and slitting his and Kate's throats, no doubt.

He gasped as a searing pain radiated from his bad arm. The one Stan broke the day Brian was killed. *Goddammit! Flares up every time I think about the Solomons! Why the hell is that?!*

It got so bad he had to stop to rub it out.

He was about to walk again when a teenage girl approached him.

—๛—

"Uh, hey there," the teen girl said, as she awkwardly approached him, sporting a curious expression on her face.

"Hello." Kevin did his best to ignore his arm, which still hurt like the blazes.

"What brings you here?"

Doesn't know who I am. "Visiting a friend." He cocked a glance up the road. "I knew the Solomons."

The teen's face fell. "You're a little late."

"I know. I heard about their son."

"You knew Brian?"

"Only in passing," Kevin said. "Did you ... know him?"

"I was his girlfriend."

Yeah, right. From what Kevin knew, there was no way this chick was Brian's girlfriend. For one thing, she dressed a little too revealing, showing her shoulders and legs in freezing weather. As though she had something to prove. *Stupid kids. So eager to show off their bodies without*

111

knowing what it means. And they wonder why they're assaulted all the damn time!

Brian Solomon always dressed casually, being in a military family and all. Everything had to be satisfactory. Can't have the military brass come to visit the family with the son dressing out of sorts.

Also, the girl was clearly a goth, with black hair, black lipstick, and guess what, dark clothes. Like one of those whiny kids who complained they had no friends before going to shoot up a school.

"Yeah, me too."

"What's your name?"

"Shirley."

"Shirley what?"

"Just Shirley," the teen answered, giving him a wary look. "And your name is?"

"Kevin Reece." He extended a hand. The handshake he got was firm. "So what's going on with their home these days?"

"No one's been in it since Brian's murder," Shirley answered. "No one has the heart to move in, and the housing company's not putting it on the market."

Murder. Kevin had to fight to keep his expression sympathetic. *Right.* "Think that'll change?"

"Nah," Shirley answered, shaking her head. "Too many folks would protest."

Of course they would, Kevin thought distastefully. *Can't people do anything else in this town besides protest?!*

—⁓—

"So," Kevin said as he walked quickly with Shirley to stay warm. *How are you not cold?!* "What can you tell me about this place?"

"Don't you already know?" the teen asked, giving him a curious eye. "You said you were a friend of the Solomons."

"Me and Stan served in the same unit during the war. I lost track of him after we were discharged."

That wasn't a total lie.

Kevin did serve in the army, but he retired earlier than Stan did.

Still felt like shit for lying, though.

It's for Kate, Kevin thought, repeating the phrase in his head to supress any doubt in his mind. *It's for Kate. It's for Kate. It's ALL for Kate.*

"He was gone for a long time," Shirley answered, seeming a little too at home with talking to a stranger. "When he came back, the neighborhood had a party. Cake, streamers, all the trimmings."

"Weren't you invited?"

"Nah, I got here a few months earlier. Hit it off with Brian, though. Mr. and Ms. Solomon came by with a pie to welcome me and my folks to the neighborhood."

"Okay," Kevin answered in a good-natured voice. *Gonna file that detail away for later.* "When Brian was killed, did anyone react to it badly? Besides the Solomons, I mean."

"More than a few," Shirley answered sadly. "The whole neighborhood loved him."

Enough to aid in kidnapping the cop who killed him? Kevin wondered. The creature that threatened him wasn't human, but it wasn't animalistic. It knew how to work a phone. "Anyone stand out?"

"Nah. Everyone was too busy consoling Ms. Solomon."

"And Stan?"

"I brought him a pie, you know?" Shirley said, a sad expression on her face. "To cheer him up. Pay him back for being so nice to me."

"How'd he act?"

"Like a dad that lost his son," she answered, giving Kevin a curt look.

"Right." *Smartass.* "Any strange activity here since?"

"Since?"

Just come out with it. "Since the trial."

"Well, Ms. Solomon was holed up in her house," Shirley answered as they came to a street crossing. Kevin stopped to look both ways while Shirley just walked straight through. "She was such a wreck after Brian's murder she had to give up her teaching job."

Stop saying murder! The pain in his arm grew worse. *It wasn't murder!* "So she had a nervous breakdown?"

"You could say that." Shirly stopped, turning slowly on her heels to face him. "You know, you don't seem very sympathetic."

113

"Sorry, just trying to paint a picture."

"Right." She stared at him, maybe sizing up his intentions.

Move on. Don't give her time to think! "What about Stan? What did he do?"

"Thanked the neighbors. Talked to the military brass that kept coming to their home."

A lot of military personnel were character witnesses during the trial. It looked as though Stan had called in every branch of the armed forces to his side.

People like that knew how to make people disappear. Maybe even how to create operatives skilled at interrogation.

Kevin had thought the creature wasn't human, but then again, he had seen it only from far away. At night. Maybe it was a regular human—a highly trained one—in some kind of crazy stealth suit. "After that, though?"

"People stopped coming."

"How'd the Solomons take that?"

"Mr. Solomon was cool with it, always was, but Ms. Solomon? It was like she dropped off the face of the earth."

Or was eaten up by that house, Kevin thought when he saw it coming up on their right.

—⟳—

"So," Shirley said as they stopped in front of the Solomons' home. "Why are you *really* here?"

"Excuse me?" Kevin rubbed his hands together, trying to keep them warm. *How are you not cold?!*

"You're a friend of Mr. Solomon's, and you come now? Almost a year after their son was murdered?" She gave Kevin an annoyed look. "Doesn't add up."

Girl's got me there. "It's best I don't tell you."

"Because?"

"Because I'm protecting you," Kevin stated in a firm yet friendly voice.

"Protecting me?" Shirley asked. "Or yourself?"

Oh come on! "Look, I'm trying to help someone in jeopardy, and I need to get in this house to do it."

"Likely story," Shirley said dismissively, pulling her phone out of her pocket. "I'm calling the police—"

"Don't do that," Kevin said quickly, putting a hand on hers. "Time's of the essence here. If I don't act now, someone very important to me might die."

Shirley, her finger on the call button, seemed to consider his words. "Okay, Mr. Reece, I'll let you go inside."

"Thank you."

"But," she added, her eyes flashing like lightning, "this family's suffered enough. So's this neighborhood. This house, the people that lived in it, they're important to us. You do *anything* to tarnish that, you'll answer to me."

"Understood," Kevin said, nodding.

"I mean that." Shirley fixed him with a threatening look before walking away.

Kevin felt an unseen power, reverberating from the walls of the Solomons' residential building as he cautiously approached the steps. *Girl's words are getting to me.* Who the hell was she to threaten him?! He was a cop, for cripes' sake, and she was just … a real pain in his ass!

Letting out a nervous breath, he stepped over the police tape and slipped inside the house.

The living room was frigid as a tundra, shocking Kevin to moments after the not-guilty verdict came down during Kate Barrow's trial.

Francine was crying in the courtroom.

Stan was simmering with anger.

The citywide riots that followed were so bad there was no time to check on them.

Sure, the neighbors did, but they were not going to tell the police anything.

If one of them had told us something, we could've prevented this, Kevin thought distastefully. *Gotten the Solomons the help they needed. And Kate would still be here.*

Sure, their son would still be dead, but nothing could change that.

—⟋Ⱳ⟍—

What am I looking for? Kevin wondered as he moved through the Solomons' home. *A witch's cauldron? A pentagram on the wall? Hell, a black cat hissing in the corner?*

Did they even own a cat?

There was no way to know how the Solomons got the abilities they displayed when they took Kate.

Or how they conjured the creature trying to scare Kevin away.

Or was there one?

He moved to Brian's bedroom. It was medium sized, with video games and posters on the wall.

Posters of comic book characters.

Here's something, Kevin thought as he approached a poster of Superman. *Didn't Drake's report say the Solomons wore a getup like this?*

Spandex and a cape with a symbol on their chests?

Did this inspire them? Kevin saw another one. *Or whoever it was who gave them their powers?*

—⟋Ⱳ⟍—

Let's see what's on Brian's desk. Kevin sat down and looked through academic awards.

An honor student. Of course he was a freaking honor student!

A piece of paper tucked in the back of a drawer caught his attention. Kevin pulled it out, careful not to tear it. *What's this?*

It was a drawing of two people, dressed like the Solomons were the night they took Kate. They even looked like Stan and Francine. Kevin glanced back at the posters. *Brian was turning his parents into analogs of his favorite superheroes. Why?*

Parental worship?

Or something more?

He turned the paper over, saw faint scratches on the back. *Hold on.* He pulled a pencil from his pocket and ran the tip lightly over the scratches, hoping the lead would catch onto the grooves.

There we go, Kevin thought as he uncovered what looked like symbols. He ran his fingers over them, the ache in his arm intensifying. He scowled, taking his hand away.

The pain subsided.

On a hunch, Kevin touched the symbols again.

The pain returned.

What the . . . Kevin repeated the motion a few times, the pain getting so bad it almost brought tears to his eyes. As he looked at his arm, then at the paper, a crazy thought came to his mind.

What if it wasn't Stan or Francine who called for those crazy powers?

What if it was Brian himself?

—⚊—

Whoa, buddy, Kevin thought, sliding the chair he sat in away from Brian's desk. *I'm gonna need proof before I can accuse the Solomons' golden boy of anything. More than a picture with a few crazy scribbles.*

Kevin leaned back in Brian's chair, rubbing his eyes. *Where would I hide evidence of wrongdoing if I were the Solomons?*

He cracked his back. *Someplace out of the way.* He then glanced up and saw the imprint of a trapdoor in the ceiling of the hallway. *Like an attic!*

Kevin got to his feet and put the paper in a plastic bag. *Save this for later.*

He pulled at the latch on the trapdoor, bringing down a staircase. *Perfect.* It touched the floor, giving him a clear way into the attic.

Kevin squared his shoulders and made the climb.

—⚊—

Looks like I got that proof I need, Kevin thought as he took in the eldritch scene before him, shock and awe on his face. *That and then some.*

The attic's walls were covered in the same symbols as the ones on the back of Brian's paper. Scribbled in black ink, they assaulted Kevin's mind, making his bad arm light up as though was on fire. It forced him to one knee, grimacing in pain.

There was no way Brian could've scribbled this. That meant that either Stan or Francine was the author of what he was seeing.

But from what Shirley told him, Stan was too busy making nice with the neighbors to have the time.

That left Francine.

But how did she know to do this?

And what was it?!

Something in her family, Kevin thought as his arm hurt like the devil's piss. *Some ancient tradition passed down through the generations.*

What was he looking at?

Magic? Sorcery?

Witchcraft?

Tearing up, Kevin took quick snapshots with his cell phone.

A sickening vertigo made the room spin. *I ... got enough*, Kevin decided as he put the phone back in his pocket. Salty tears streamed down his face, reducing everything to murky shadows and shapes.

Including one that was ... coming right at him?!

"I warned you." A fist shot out, catching Kevin across the face. "I warned you."

The blow sent him spinning into the opposite wall. He hit it hard, the symbols slashing his clothes like knives. *Goddammit!*

He slid to the floor, the room still spinning.

The Solomons' creature darted out of the shadows, picking Kevin up and flinging him against another wall.

It let him drop, the impact leaving cracks in the wood.

His back aching, his bad arm burning like a poker, Kevin looked up at his attacker. *Jesus Christ, it looks worse up close!*

It was big, with shoulders and hands way too big for its body. It was clothed in white scales that reflected the light in strange colors.

It came at Kevin again, kicking him through a window.

Kevin found himself flailing through cold air, managing to brace himself before landing in the front yard.

He smacked his head, momentarily seeing stars.

Have to get out of here. Kevin gingerly got to his feet, a flickering light drawing his attention back to the Solomons' house …

Which was going up in flames!

Shit, I was just *in there!* His eyes widened in shock as he watched neighbors running out of their homes. The horror on their faces turned to anger as they turned their gaze on him.

"No," Kevin whispered, shaking his head. "No …"

"You did this …"

"No …"

"You're that cop!"

"Wait," Kevin said as the neighbors surrounded him. "Listen! Please listen!"

"Call the police!"

I am the police! Kevin ran for it, firing his gun in the air to break up a crowd that was quickly becoming a lynch mob.

The smarter neighbors let him pass.

The bolder ones threw things at him.

"Arrgh!" A glass bottle clocked Kevin in the back of the head, dashing him to the ground. Goddammit! As he scrambled to his feet, he saw Shirley, standing in front of the towering inferno that was the Solomon home.

The look of betrayal on her pale face shook him to his soul.

Crying tears of pain from his arm and multiple injuries, Kevin got to his car. He had only seconds to whip out his keys, get his driver-side door open, and jump inside. He started the car and shot out of the neighborhood like a bat out of hell.

—ᴍ—

Can't go home, Kevin realized as his vision grew blurry. *Isenguard will be waiting for me.* And there was no way Madsen would let him off this time. *Have to* …

Everything went black for a second, Kevin narrowly missing plowing into a tree. He stopped the car. *Have to get off the road!*

He patted his phone, remembering the pictures. That creature was covering the Solomons' tracks. Kevin didn't understand much about any of this, but he understood that.

But he couldn't keep driving, not in his condition.

He had to get someplace safe. Clear his head.

Someplace out of the way.

He couldn't get to Joan now, not with the creature watching his every move.

And Ms. Barrow? That was *definitely* a no-go!

He felt his phone in his pocket vibrate. *Shit!* Grimacing in pain, he put the receiver to his ear. "Hello?!"

"What did you do?!"

Ms. Barrow! "I had no choice."

"The GCPD's after you! You're a suspect in the Solomon house fire!"

Man, they work fast. "How do you know that?"

"You think I can't work a dispatch radio?"

"Right." Kevin took in a deep breath, willing back the pain.

"Where are you?"

"On the outskirts of town." Kevin looked around. "Near the freeway, the I-5." *I put no thought into where I was going!*

"The I-5," Ms. Barrow said. "That's near Milestone City. You thinking of running?"

"You thinking of coming to get me?"

"You damn right I am."

"Might not be a good idea," Kevin said.

"Don't you *dare* shut me out now. My daughter's still missing."

"Yeah, and I got a freaking demon on my ass," Kevin shot back. "It caused the fire."

"Dear lord."

"It's tying up loose ends, Ms. Barrow." After a long bit of silence, he added. "I'm one of those loose ends."

The implication of those words must have hit her, because there was silence on the line. Then soft whispering. Then curse words.

"Ms. Barrow?" *C'mon, woman, talk to me!*

"You need to come in," she said. "Just come clean! Madsen will protect you!"

"I did earlier," Kevin answered wistfully. "He wants this case closed."

Ms. Barrow's voice grew thick with emotion. "We can't just give up!"

"We're not going to. You got a computer where you are?"

"I … yes."

"Stay by it. I'll get to a hotel, get on a computer. I got pictures to send to you."

"Kevin …" Ms. Barrow paused, perhaps racking her brain for the right thing to say. "Don't do anything crazy, okay? It's not over yet."

Kevin looked back the way he came. He thought he saw a shape in the distance. "Not over yet."

Kevin ended the call and was about to start his car when his phone vibrated again. *What now?* He picked up the phone. "I told you to—"

"You son of a bitch."

He blinked, the words taking him completely by surprise. "Shirley?"

"Who do you think, jackass?"

Alarms going off in his head, Kevin gripped the phone tight. "How'd you get this number?"

"How could you set fire to the Solomons' home like that?!"

"That wasn't me!"

"Likely story," she spat. "These people have been through enough pain, and you just piled it on, didn't' you? And worse, you made me a part of it!"

"Shirley, listen to me," Kevin began. "I didn't set the fire. You have to believe me."

"Like I had to believe you're a friend of the Solomons, Officer Jacobson?"

Shit, Kevin thought, his heart sinking in his chest. There was no way she would believe him now. He had made nothing but bad decisions ever since taking this case.

Each one worse than the last.

"Nothing to say now?"

Taking a deep breath, Kevin answered. "Shirley, listen to me. There's more going on here than you think—than anyone thinks. I hope one day you'll see that."

"That's all you have to tell me?! I loved Brian! And you let your partner kill him!"

"I know, Shirley," Kevin said, feeling like Christ on the cross. "I never meant for that to happen. For *any* of this to happen." *That sounds so sappy!* "But sometimes ... things get out of control. You'll see, when you're older."

"The cops are after you," came the confident reply. "I helped them. We *all* did."

"I know," Kevin said, the words pitiful to his ears.

"They'll catch you," she continued as though she hadn't heard anything. "And when they do, I hope you get what's coming to you."

Looking back the way he came, Kevin was sure he would.

One way or another.

—⁂—

With the clarity of a man heading to the gallows, Kevin drove to the first hotel he came across. A dingy one on the edge of town.

Motel 6 or something.

He paid with cash, taking care to avoid the clerk's direct gaze. He saw that the one TV in the lobby was tuned to the World Cup. A group of people surrounded it, partying and talking about their favorite teams.

He envied their comradery.

Without any emotion, he asked if the room had Wi-Fi.

The clerk, maybe tipped off by his tone, said it was an extra five bucks.

Kevin paid the fee, took his key, and limped to his room.

—⁘—

Few more things to wrap up, Kevin thought as he opened the photo app on his phone. He linked all the pictures into a file and sent it to Ms. Barrow's phone via text message. He smiled when he saw it had gotten through. *Good enough.*

With Shirley's words rattling in his head, he dialed Joan's number.

He knew she would be working late again, but he wanted to leave a message.

"Hey, this is Joan," her machine said. "You know what to do."

The beep that came after was like a death bell.

Wish we had more time. "Hey babe. I … I know you're mad at me. And you got good reason …" Kevin paused, wiping a tear from his eye. "You're gonna hear some bad things about me. From everyone. I want you to know they're not true." He paused again. "Well, some of them are true."

He closed his eyes, deciding to let it all out. "When I let that kid die … I put a mark on me. I never told you. Didn't want it to touch you." He let out a sigh, feeling the weight of regret. "You're the best thing in my life. Whatever happens … please, *please*, believe that."

He hung up the phone, slid it under the bed, and turned to the door.

He took out his gun and checked the chamber.

Taking a firing position, he pointed it at the door, finger on the trigger. *Come on, you son of a bitch. Come on!*

—⁘—

Shirley Alexander looked sadly upon the Solomon house as firefighters did their best to put out the flames. It was slow going since the flames didn't die.

If that wasn't strange enough, they affected only the Solomons' house!

—⁘—

Joan Collins sat at her desk, another late night under her belt. She had spent the last few hours thinking about her argument with Kevin.

He had a good heart but was such an idiot sometimes!

This isn't the Wild West, Joan thought when she heard a noise from down the hall. Cautiously, she got up to check it out. *The Wild West wasn't the Wild Test!*

She stopped, looking down an empty hall. *Could've sworn I heard something.* She looked back to her office.

Kevin *did* say something was stalking him.

—⟞⟝—

Had Joan gone back to her office right then, she would have seen the very creature Kevin had been talking about.

It stood at her desk, eyes narrowing as it made a decision.

Then something made it change that decision.

It turned to the window, smirked as only it could, and left the building out of a nearby window.

—⟞⟝—

A bone-chilling screech rocked Motel 6 a few minutes later, waking guests from their revelry.

The gunshots that followed got the staff to call the police.

Crime scene investigators from the GCPD traced the shots to the recently rented room of Officer Kevin Jacobson, a suspect in a fire that destroyed the Solomon house.

Upon entering the room, police officers saw Jacobson's spent handgun cooling on top of the bed, three bullet holes in the wall near the door.

Yet despite clear evidence of a struggle, there was no sign of Jacobson himself.

—⟞⟝—

Ms. Barrow—Jennifer to her friends—got Kevin's message and the package attached to it. Hooking her phone to her laptop, she downloaded the package and opened it.

It revealed pictures Kevin had taken of the inside of the Solomons' attic.

Wincing at the craziness of the content, Jennifer rubbed her eyes, counted to 10, and then gave the pictures her full attention.

She could work with this. She *would* work with this.

It wasn't her daughter, safe and sound. But it was a start.

It was a start.

BARROW'S RISING

ood Lord! Jennifer Barrow stared at a set of photos in utter disbelief. *What am I even supposed to do with this?* A hardboiled and steely-eyed mother of two, she sat in a hotel room in the heart of Gateway City, holding a steaming cup of coffee in her hands as she tried to decipher the photos that sat on her table.

Officer Kevin Jacobson, a new recruit in her quest to find her daughter, had sent them to her a few minutes ago.

Her daughter's name was Kate Barrow.

A police officer herself, she was kidnapped a few days ago by a crazed couple—Stan and Francine Solomon—for killing their son in the line of duty.

Now Officer Jacobson wasn't returning her phone calls.

And all she had to go on to save her daughter were photos of manic scrawling on the walls of the Solomons' house!

—◊—

Detective Julie Benz arrived at the Motel 6, just outside of Gateway City. She had her game face on and was dressed in plain clothes, her dark brown hair pulled back in an efficient ponytail.

She carefully stepped past the crime scene investigators as they processed the scene of Officer Jacobson's kidnapping for clues. *This is getting out of control.*

"Detective," the head analyst called out as she stood outside Jacobson's hotel room.

"Willows. How are things?"

"Grim," the analyst answered quietly. He wore a CSI jacket and a dark baseball cap. Weariness colored his features, his gray eyes matching his hair. "Getting real tired of processing people I know."

"Can I come in?"

"Of course, though I hear you weren't assigned to this case."

"I'm not," Benz said as she stepped into the room, careful to keep out of the way. "Technically, I'm still on leave."

"It's bad, Benz." Willows handed her a pair of plastic gloves. "Real bad."

"I don't see signs of a struggle," she said, quietly scanning the room.

"We got blood, but only on the bed." Willows pointed at the single bed in the dingy hotel room. "A few drops on the covers. A few more fell on the floor at the foot of the bed. Not enough to indicate a struggle, though."

"Whose blood is it?"

"Jacobson's."

"Damn."

"I know, right?" Willows pointed at the door. "See the space next to it?"

"I do," Benz answered, following his gesture. "I also see the bullet holes."

"That is the only evidence we have that something shady happened here. "That and the fact that Jacobson's gone."

"Anything on his attacker?"

"According to the evidence, there *was no* attacker."

That got a surprised look from Benz. "What?"

"I know it's strange. But we have no evidence that anyone was in this room except Jacobson."

"For God's sake, Willows. He couldn't have kidnapped himself."

"You know that, and I know that. But that's not what the evidence is showing me."

His kidnapper knows how to cover his tracks, Benz thought darkly. *So much that even seasoned CSIs can't find them. That shows intellect, ingenuity, and the ability to manipulate the environment around them.*

Those were the same qualities the Solomons showed the night they took Kate while she and her partner watched helplessly.

—∞—

Slow down, Jennifer thought, massaging her temples. *Don't lose your head. You can't bring Kate home if you lose your head.*

She stood up from the table, needing a break. *Better call room service.* She checked the clock. *They should still be open. It's only a little after nine.*

But first, she turned on the TV.

—∞—

"Benz," Willows said, stepping close to her so no one else could hear. "Could this case be —*gulp!* — Solomons related?"

"Possibly," he answered. "Jacobson was Kate Barrow's partner when she killed Brian Solomon. Stan and Francine Solomon saw him at the scene. Stan even got in an altercation with him and broke his arm. And Jacobson was present at Kate's trial as a character witness."

"Yeah," Benz admitted. "He was."

"I heard his testimony got the jury to side with her. That true?"

"You're asking me?"

"Yes, I am," Willows answered. "The higher-ups aren't telling us anything. My boys are getting scared, and so am I."

"The whole GCPD's scared," Benz admitted. "Not just of the Solomons but of what would come next."

Kate Barrow's not-guilty verdict had plunged Gateway City into a riot that resulted in a million dollars in damage and fifty-five people dead.

Everyone was afraid Stan and Francine could kick off another one, especially with their kidnapping victim being a cop.

That and they had freaking superpowers!

—∞—

The first thing Jennifer saw was the headline: DISGRACED COP
DISAPPEARS.

Oh no. With a shaking hand, she turned up the volume on the TV.

"Officer Kevin Jacobson is the latest in a rash of disappearances
that have plagued Gateway City since the abduction of Officer Kate
Barrow. Last seen at a Motel 6, Jacobson worked as Barrow's partner, a
controversial figure since the shooting death of a teenaged boy named
Brian Solomon."

Do they have to focus on that Solomon kid? Jennifer stared at the TV
in disbelief. *Kevin just went missing, for God's sake!*

"While law enforcement officials aren't ruling this a kidnapping, the
timing of Jacobson's disappearance is too suspicious to ignore, given that
he was present at the scene of Brian Solomon's shoot—"

Jennifer switched off the TV and then sat on the bed, head in her
hands. *The Solomons took him too! All because he was trying to help me!* She
raised her head, a look of determination on her face. *Means I got two
people to bring home now.*

—m—

"Are you on this case?" Willows asked.

"Kind of," Benz admitted. "It's complicated."

"But not sanctioned."

"How'd you—?"

"Because Drake's your partner, and he's not here," Willows answered.
"You two are usually a package deal."

"He's with his family," Benz said. "On convalescence leave.
Technically, so am I."

"So you're a concerned citizen, now?"

"You could say that."

"Good," a stern voice said from the doorway. "Then as a 'concerned
citizen,' you can leave my crime scene."

Dammit. Benz turned on her heels to see a giant, dressed in plain
clothes, blocking her only way out of the hotel room. "Hello, Inspector
Isenguard."

Everyone looked away, not eager to get between the two of them.

"Uh, yeah," Willows said. "Think I'll leave you with him." He took a step back, looking for business elsewhere.

"Hello, Detective Benz," Isenguard said with measured civility. "You're a long way from home. Which is where you should be. *Your* home."

"Gateway City's my home," Benz said, refusing to back down. "Every bit of it."

"Then why don't I escort you to some OTHER part of it?" Isenguard motioned for her to follow him. "Right now?"

—⚎—

Drops of blood fell from Jennifer's nose as she looked over Kevin's photos again. A minute later, it dripped from her ears.

Enough! She closed the folder containing the images, afraid of what would happen if she looked at them a second longer. The symbols flashed before her eyes, as if taunting her.

Get out! She manically ran her fingers through her hair. *Get out!*

—⚎—

"You're not taking me to my apartment," Benz remarked, recognizing the landmarks Isenguard passed not being anywhere near her neighborhood.

"You're an astute observer," Isenguard said as he made a right turn.

Thanks for the compliment. "May I ask *why* we're not going to my apartment?"

"Why were you at the crime scene?" the giant detective asked as he kept his eyes on the road ahead of them. "And no lies. I can smell a liar."

I want to believe he's pulling my leg, Benz thought as she shot Isenguard a quizzical look. *But I've heard too many stories.* "I'm trying to bring Kate home. To do that, I need to talk to the Solomons. I was hoping to talk to Jacobson at the hotel. Maybe compare notes with him."

"And you decided to get involved, now?"

131

Is he trying to guilt me? "I would have acted sooner," she said sarcastically, "but I was busy healing after the Solomons dropped a freaking lightning bolt on my head."

"Good point," Isenguard said, cracking his shoulders. It was comical seeing him squirm in a squad car too small for him. He was a whopping seven foot three, but with the GCPD under budget, getting him a height-appropriate vehicle was a challenge. So he got used to scrunching his shoulders whenever he needed to drive.

Benz, meanwhile, was completely comfortable, at five feet eight, riding in the passenger seat. Her slim frame gave her plenty of room to move. She liked to think her size was the reason the Solomons' lightning bolt didn't hurt her despite decimating Kate Barrow's home.

The problem was that didn't leave her any strength to stop the Solomons from taking Kate. And they were out there, doing who knows what to her.

Her and Jacobson!

—⁂—

A few harrowing minutes later, Jennifer looked up from her hands. Her vision had cleared, and she saw only a few drops of blood at her feet. *I'm building up a tolerance. Not sure that's a good thing.*

She pushed that defeatist thought away.

I'll stay here for tonight. She would need the rest. The next leg was North Carolina, clear on the other side of the country.

That would be a hell of a drive.

Can't think about that, Jennifer thought desperately. *I can't even entertain the notion of defeat. Not until Kate and Jacobson are home.*

—⁂—

"The Solomons are cleaning house, Isenguard," Benz declared as Isenguard continued driving the two of them through Gateway City's streets.

"I know."

"First Kate, then Jacobson. They're going after every person they hold responsible for Brian's death." She checked her watch, saw it was six in the morning. The sun would be up soon. "That could extend to every person that led to Kate's not-guilty verdict."

"I know that too," Isenguard agreed as he turned a corner. "We got the judge and every member of the jury that oversaw their case under protection."

"Why didn't Kevin get that same courtesy?"

"Chief Madsen felt he didn't need it."

That's bull. "Really? For Christ's sake, he was Kate's partner! You're telling me it never occurred to the chief that he might be next?"

"I only know what I'm told, Benz," Isenguard said as he pulled his squad car to a stoplight. "And believe me, I brought it up."

"And let me guess, he said no."

"That he did."

Benz sighed, leaning back in her seat. "So where are we going?"

"To Doubletree Inn," Isenguard answered as the light turned green. "We got someone to see."

"Anyone that can help us?"

"We'll see," he answered as he put his foot on the gas, their car rocketing down the street.

—⟊—

Harsh knocking woke Jennifer from her slumber, the symbols from the photos dancing across her groggy vision.

Who? She looked to a clock on her nightstand, saw it was 8:00 a.m. *Only been two hours?* She sat up gingerly, her body laden with aches and pains. *When'd I get to bed? I was at the table, last I remember ...*

Swinging her legs over the side of the bed, she stood on shaky feet. The room spun before her eyes.

Fuck me. She never used to curse before Kate's kidnapping. Funny what changes a few months could make.

The knocking started again, this time more insistent.

"I'm coming!" Jennifer waited for the room to right itself, then stumbled. "I'm coming!" *Who's knocking at this hour?!* "Okay, what's going—" She opened the door, only to gasp as a giant in a trench coat blocked the entrance.

"Greetings, Mrs. Barrow," the giant said amicably. "I'm Inspector Isenguard." He motioned to a woman behind him, who had to stand on tiptoes to be seen. "This here is Detective Benz. We'd like to talk to you about the disappearance of Kevin Jacobson."

"Uh …" *How'd they find me?*

Isenguard calmly waved his badge. "And we're gonna have to insist."

—✦—

So this is Jennifer Barrow, Benz thought as she looked at the woman sitting on the bed in front of them. *Doesn't look like much. Of course, I'm sure folks say the same thing about me.*

And who looked like a movie star, first thing in the morning?

"So," she said, trying to sound casual, "you guys finally decided to get involved, eh?"

"We've always been involved, Mrs. Barrow," Isenguard said patiently.

"Funny, that's the same thing your chief said when I asked him about finding my little girl."

"And we're still looking for her. We told you this when you came by the station. Every day, for months."

"And yet here you are, harassing me because one of your guys went missing," Mrs. Barrow spat. "Hasn't even been gone twenty-four hours, and here you are."

"We're just following police procedure, ma'am."

"How'd you find me?"

"You paid for this room with your credit card," Isenguard answered, "the second you did that, we knew where to find you."

"Crap," Mrs. Barrow swore, massaging the bridge of her nose. "Should've known *that* was gonna happen."

"Had a long night, Mrs. Barrow?" Benz cut in finally. *I'm sorry Isenguard, but we don't have time for subtlety.*

—✦—

Who is this? Jennifer turned to the young woman. "And who are you?"

"Detective Julie Benz," Benz answered, holding out her hand.

"Right, right, he just told me ..." *C'mon, Jen! Wake up!*

"I was present when your daughter was taken."

"You ..." Jennifer's eyes widened at the gravity of her words. "You were ... ?"

"Yes, Mrs. Barrow," she said, nodding. "I'm sorry I didn't do enough to get her back to you."

"It's not your—" A bitter taste then settled in the back of Jennifer's throat as a sudden realization came to her. "Why didn't you ...? Why didn't you save Kate?!"

"I tried," Detective Benz said, in a patient voice, cutting her off quickly. "I'm still trying. I need you to believe that."

"You need me to *believe*?!" Jennifer finally got her lips to move. "Why the hell didn't you try harder?!"

"The Solomons have powers, Mrs. Barrow. Superpowers."

"You're *police officers*!"

"We're not gods, Mrs. Barrow," Isenguard said sternly, leaning forward. "If the last few months have taught us anything, it's that."

"You people can do anything! Why the hell didn't you protect my daughter?!"

"I could ask you why your 'daughter' shot an innocent fifteen-year-old boy in the line of duty, if you really want to pursue this line of questioning." Isenguard's eyes narrowed. "Who taught her it was okay to do *that*, I wonder?"

How dare you! Jennifer's eyes were like knives. "Don't insult how I raise my child because you people can't do your jobs!"

"Mrs. Barrow, recriminations like these will get us nowhere," Benz said, putting a hand on the big detective's shoulder. "Most likely, this is what the Solomons want."

Jennifer rose to say more, but seeing the young woman's no-nonsense face put out her fire. It was clear from the look in her eyes that she was haunted. That she had seen things the night Kate was taken. "All right, fine. But *only* if you're here to help."

The giant inspector grunted dismissively, cracking his knuckles. "I take it you heard about Jacobson's disappearance."

"Yeah, I heard about it," Jennifer said reluctantly. "Still can't believe it."

"We know you were working with him," Isenguard declared. "He told us himself. Said it was to help you get Barrow back."

"Kate," Jennifer hissed through gritted teeth. "Her name is Kate. Kate. Barrow."

"As you *keep* telling us," Isenguard said, giving her a dismissive look.

Just like James, Jennifer thought, remembering her husband. He gave her that look too, though he had the good grace to try to hide it. A look that said she was crazy or, worse, emotional. All because she refused to see their daughter's kidnapping as "part of the job."

To see that same look on the face of someone who was supposed to be Kate's brother in arms rankled her to no end. She wanted to deck the smug giant, but she knew she would be arrested for assault.

"Sir," Detective Benz asked, taking him by the shoulder, "could I speak to you for a minute?"

—∞—

"Sir," Benz said as they stood in the hall outside of Mrs. Barrow's room. "We need to reconsider our approach."

"Our approach?" Isenguard asked, looking down his nose at her. "This is my investigation."

"Then why'd you call me here?"

"To consult."

Do not pull this crap on me now. "Inspector …"

"I know how you and Detective Drake do things," Isenguard continued, turning his body to fully face her. "And I get that he tolerates your insubordination, but I don't. I'm your superior, you're my subordinate. You cut me off like that again; I will send you back home." He leaned close to her face, his countenance all business. "And I will make sure you stay there."

"Do you want to bring Kate home?" Benz met his stern expression with her own. "Or do you want to waste time peacocking?"

That took Isenguard aback. "Excuse me?"

No wonder you're Chief Madsen's second in command. You're an ass, just like him. "You're treating Mrs. Barrow like a perp while we need her as an ally."

"We need her to quit giving us sass."

Sass? Benz's eyes widened in disbelief. *Who says that about a grown woman?* "And acting like a bully's not going to make that happen. From what I heard, you and Chief Madsen acted this way with Jacobson too. How'd that go?"

The hardness seemed to leave Isenguard's eyes. He sighed, looking down at his shoes. "I see your point."

About time! "Thank you, sir."

"How do you want to play this?"

"Let me talk to her," Benz answered in a tactful voice. "She responds to me."

"She backtalks you more than she does me."

"She wants to blow off steam. We let her do that, she'll be as docile as a kitten." Benz knew her words could sound condescending to the wrong person, but she had to get Isenguard on her side. And men like him listened to boastful words.

They considered them a sign of strength.

Frank had told her as much on her first day riding with him.

"Okay," Isenguard said, letting out a reluctant breath. "We'll play it your way. But remember this, I'm going out on a limb here. No one from the station knows we're even here. Not Chief Madsen, not the DA. It's just us. We need to be on the same page."

"Thank you," Benz said, turning back to the door to Mrs. Barrow's room. "Please stay out here. I'll go in and talk to her. Give me a few minutes."

"Very well. I'll text you from time to time. To make sure you're okay."

Huh? Benz's brow arched in surprise. "You think she's going to attack me?"

"She's Kate's mother, Benz. And she's desperate. We don't know *what* she'll do."

—⁂—

Wasting time, Jennifer thought, keeping her gaze on the door to keep from pacing around her hotel room. Or screaming in frustration. *Why'd I shout at them? I need them to find Kate!*

Her knees bounced nervously as she waited for the detectives to return. All she could do was think of her little Kate. *We used to call her Kitty when she was younger ...*

Like when she went to her senior prom ...

Or when she tried out for her high school football team. A boys' team, believe it or not. *Should've known then she wasn't going to be like the other girls. No, being normal wasn't good enough for her!*

When she told Jennifer and James that she wanted to be cop, it was more of a confirmation than a surprise. *We tried to talk her out of it, but she wouldn't hear us.*

And where was she now?

Moving away from me, Jennifer thought as she put a hand on her knee to keep it from bouncing. *Is Kitty with Kevin? Or is she with the monsters that took him?*

Benz stepped back into the room, seeing that Mrs. Barrow had moved from the bed to the very seat she had been sitting in during their round of questions. The beleaguered mother looked up at her with wary eyes. Benz could tell from the slight pinkish hue that she had been crying. *Looks like seeing me drudged up some memories.* "Do you want a tissue?" she asked, pulling a folded tissue from her jacket pocket.

"No, thank you," Mrs. Barrow answered, sniffing a bit. "I'm sorry I blew up at you, earlier. It's just ..."

"You're frustrated. I get it." Benz paused, reconsidering her answer. "I feel for you."

"I tried talking to your partner, Detective Drake."

"I know," Benz said, sitting in the chair opposite her. "He told me during his rehabilitation."

"Where is he now anyway?"

"At home. With his family. Recuperating."

"At least someone's with their family."

Benz scanned the room, her gaze fixed on a file sitting on top of a desk across from the bed. "Mrs. Barrow, what did Officer Jacobson send to you before he disappeared?"

"Pictures."

"Of?"

"The Solomons' home," Mrs. Barrow answered.

Wow. Bent's brow arched in surprise. "He went inside?"

"He did. I told him to wait for me, but he went alone. He said it was to protect me, but I think he was just being macho." Mrs. Barrows shifted uncomfortably in her chair. "Seems like everyone in this cursed city would rather put on a façade than do their jobs."

"You have no idea," Benz agreed. "I'm sure your daughter saw her fair share, being a woman on the force."

"I told her not to do it," Mrs. Barrow said. "I warned her. Begged her. I told her, 'It'll use you up.'" Her eyes narrowed in resentment. "They'll chew you up, then spit you out, broken and bleeding." She swallowed, a faint hiccup escaping her lips. "Just didn't think 'they' would be parents like me."

"The Solomons are many things, but they're not like you."

"Oh, but they are," Mrs. Barrow corrected sadly. "They're parents who've lost a child, just like me. Had him taken away from them by someone they trusted. And just like me, they're trying to get him back. In their own way."

—☜—

Jennifer almost chuckled as Detective Benz did a double take. *Keep it together, girl.*

"Wait a minute." Benz gazed at Jennifer with a curious expression. "You empathize with the Solomons?"

"'Empathize' is a strong word," she said, leaning close to her. "I just … understand where they're coming from. A parent's first obligation, their privilege, is their child's safety. And when that safety's compromised, they will do anything to bring hell to the one that compromised it. That's what they did to my little girl." Jennifer leaned back. "I'd do the same in their shoes."

139

"Didn't expect that answer."

"Oh, don't get me wrong," Jennifer continued. "I'm getting my little girl back. But the way to fight an enemy is to understand how they think."

Benz nodded. "I get that."

"I know you do," Jennifer said, giving the young detective a once-over. "So knowing that, I gotta ask. How far are you willing to go to help me bring my little girl home?"

Benz didn't flinch. "As far as I need to—"

"That's good to hear."

"Without compromising myself."

"And if your boss objects?" Jennifer cocked her head at the door to her hotel room. "Or has … other ideas?"

"I'm not going to go against him," Benz answered. "But I'll convince him otherwise. He's the reason I'm here, right now."

"I see." *Good to know.*

"He wants Kate back, same as us."

"we want Kate back," Jennifer corrected in a stern voice. "*He* just wants to protect his precious boys' club. They all do."

"Then 'they' don't have to know what we're doing," Benz said, her voice warm and tender. "All right?"

After a few minutes of silence, Jennifer sighed, pointing to the file on her desk. "All right, Detective. Let's work together. But keep your boss out of my way."

—⁂—

"Good lord," Isenguard said, rubbing his eyes after looking over Jacobson's photos. "The Solomons did *that* to their own attic?"

"Got a splitting headache, Inspector?" Mrs. Barrow asked with false concern.

"Nothing I can't handle, Mrs. Barrow."

"Heh."

"We need to have linguistics look at these," Benz cut in, looking over the symbols herself. *How did the Solomons even know to make these? And what do they mean?* She could feel the symbols scratching at her mind, like a sharp blade carving into a block of wood. She blinked rapidly, as if trying to get something out of her eye. *Stay focused, Julie.* "They can give us a better idea of what they mean."

"I have a better idea," Mrs. Barrow cut in. "We go straight to the horse's mouth."

Benz and Isenguard turned to stare at her.

"You got a line to the Solomons?" Isenguard asked after sharing a wary glance with Benz. "You?"

"If I had that, why would I need you two?"

"Easy, Mrs. Barrow," Isenguard growled. "We're here to help."

"I mean, we need to see their parents," she explained. "More accurately, Stan's parents."

"That ... makes sense," Benz agreed, nodding her head. "When they attacked Kate, Francine told me her parents hadn't spoken to her since she married Stan. But what makes you think Stan's parents know what the symbols mean?"

"I did some research of my own into Stan's family," Mrs. Barrow answered. "Turns out they have a history of ... paranormal occurrences, going back a hundred years."

"Paranormal," Isenguard said. "Are you talking aliens? UFOs and such?"

"Given what I've seen the Solomons do, we can't dismiss anything." Benz rubbed her eyes, the faint throbbing of a headache just behind them. "But why his father, specifically?"

"Because I learned he was close to Stan when he was a kid, even during his time in the military," Mrs. Barrow answered. "And I'm betting he still is. Stan might have even talked to him after he was changed by ... whatever changed him and his wife. I'm hoping if we talk to Stan's father, we can get him to contact his son."

"That's a hell of a big *if*," Isenguard said. "When Kate was first taken, we spoke to him."

"You did?" Mrs. Barrow asked, a look of surprise on her face.

"Yeah. He came down to attend his grandson's funeral. Stayed for a while too to help Stan with the house."

"I read about that," Benz said, looking at the photos again. *Huh, doesn't hurt as much this time.* "That wasn't the only reason he came down, right?"

"Nope," Isenguard answered. "He also came to help with Stan's wife."

—ɯ—

Francine Solomon. Jennifer sat up a little straighter in her seat, the name like the sound of a gunshot in her mind. *She's who I really got to worry about.* "What happened to her?"

"Supposedly, she went a little batty after Brian Solomon was shot," Isenguard said, standing like a statue where he was. "Losing your child will do that to you."

"I know the feeling," came the solemn reply.

"Yeah, I'll bet you do," Isenguard said as he stuck a toothpick in his mouth.

Just like James, Jennifer thought, remembering how her husband did the same when he was nervous. Or trying to problem-solve. *Too bad he's not here helping to solve* this *problem!*

"Reportedly, Francine never left her house after Brian's death," Detective Benz said, looking up from the images. "Not even to report to work. The principal in the school she worked in put her on administrative leave after a conversation with Stan."

Nice to see someone's husband is supportive! "What about Randal Solomon?"

"Reportedly, he stayed for a week after the funeral but left right after. After a rather heated discussion with Stan."

"We need to speak to him," Jennifer said quickly. "I have to believe he can lead us to Stan. At the very least, arrange a sit-down with him."

"Mrs. Barrow, the Solomons don't do sit-downs," Isenguard said. "Unless they're to break bones."

"And purge cops they don't like," Benz added softly. "Which seems to be all of us."

"I have to hope they will for me," Jennifer said. "It's the only way to get my daughter back."

—m—

"And how do these symbols," Benz asked, looking at the scribbles in Jacobson's photos, "figure into your plan?" *Are some of these carved into the walls? How did Francine even do that?*

"I'm hoping Randal can tell me what they mean," Mrs. Barrow answered. "He has to!"

She sounds so desperate, Benz thought, her heart breaking for the beleaguered mother. She didn't want to damper her spirits, but she didn't see how talking to Stan's father was going to help. For all she knew, it might make things worse. She didn't see how, but that didn't mean it couldn't happen!

Besides that, Benz had nothing else to go on. She had exhausted every lead she had, and she couldn't keep visiting the Solomons' crime scenes hoping a solution would fall out of the sky. "Then we go."

"Excuse me?" Isenguard asked from where he was sitting.

"We go with her plan," Benz repeated, a touch of annoyance in her voice. "We head to North Carolina, and we see Randal Solomon face-to-face. And hope for the best."

"If you're going to leave the city, I can't go with you," the giant detective said. "Chief Madsen's expecting me back at the station tomorrow morning."

"So you can do what?" Mrs. Barrow asked sarcastically. "Rub his shoulders, pat his head, and tell him he's a good boy who's better than everybody else?"

"Mrs. Solomon," Benz cautioned. *He's my boss, woman!*

"Woman," Isenguard said, taking menacing steps toward Jennifer, "you are really starting to try my patience."

"What are you gonna do?" Mrs. Barrow asked, looking like she enjoyed goading him on. "Arrest me?"

"I can drum up a few charges."

"Sir!" Benz got in front of him, shooting Mrs. Barrow a look of incredulous alarm. *What are you? Nuts?!* "I can go with her!"

Isenguard stopped, towering over her. "Huh?"

"Like you said, I'm still on leave," Benz continued, making sure he kept his eyes on her. "No one's gonna notice me gone. Hell, the precinct might enjoy me taking a little vacation."

His expression brightened a bit. "You *are* becoming a headache, hanging around crime scenes like a freaking ghoul."

Thanks, sir, she thought disparagingly. "I can go with her, see Randal face-to-face, without the GCPD being officially involved!"

"Giving us deniability," Isenguard reasoned, a reluctant smile playing across his craggy face. "I'll allow it." He headed for the door. "Keep me in the loop."

Good lord, he bought it. "No problem, sir," Benz said, looking over her shoulder to give Mrs. Barrow a sly smile. "I guess you and me are going to need some plane tickets, Mrs. Barrow."

"After a performance like that, you can call me Jennifer."

"Well then, Jennifer, let's get online and get some plane tickets to North Carolina."

"Durham, North Carolina," Jennifer corrected. "Randal Solomon lives in Durham, North Carolina. The good ole South."

—◊◊◊—

"I can't find a single article on the Solomons," Jennifer declared as she flipped through a newspaper at a busy airport the next day. "They've been active for days, and no front-page story? How's that possible?"

"The GCPD's keeping mum on them," Benz answered as she took a seat next to her at the terminal, munching on a honey bun.

"But they're out there! You've seen them! You, your partner, your entire police squad, *saw* them!"

"That squad answers to a chain of command. And that chain of command is 'advising' all of us to stay quiet."

"The politics in this blow my mind," Jennifer muttered, shaking her head in disgust. *Can't* believe *my daughter chose to serve in this city!* "Everyone's just trying to cover their own asses instead of solving the problem!"

"I agree," Benz said, waiting for their flight to be called over the loudspeaker. "That's why I'm doing this … off the books, so to speak."

"Speaking of that, Detective," Jennifer said, a genuine grateful expression on her face. "I want to thank you for helping me. For putting up with me too, especially around your superior. That couldn't have been easy."

Goes from cussing out my police force to thanking me, Benz thought, hiding her surprise. *Woman turns on a dime.* "Come to think of it, it really wasn't. But you're welcome."

"First Jacobson, now you. The both of you willing to help me find my little girl. I'm honestly not sure it's worth it some days."

"Really?"

"I'm not blind, Detective. I see the toll this is taking on you guys," Jennier explained in a quiet voice. "I know Jacobson had a girlfriend." *And here I am, speaking about him in the past tense.*

"That he does," Benz said quietly.

"I haven't even had time to console her. Or the opportunity," Jennifer kept her gaze on the floor, ashamed to meet Benz's eyes. "She must think me a slimy opportunist. And given my actions? She'd be right."

"You're a mother looking out for her child."

"But how much of an excuse is *that*? The Solomons are doing the same thing, taking my little girl for killing their little boy. I use that logic, I'm no better than they are." Jennifer looked up, desperation in her eyes. "And I have to be better than them, Detective. I have to be. It's the only way I'm gonna get Katie back."

"North Carolina's hot," Jennifer complained as Benz drove their rental car through the streets of Durham, a day later. "Too hot, if you ask me."

"I don't know," she said. "At least the Solomons aren't here."

That we know of, Jennifer thought as she wiped sweat from her brow. *Stay focused, Jennie. We're here for one reason.*

"What's Randal's address again?"

"It's 2716 Campus Walk Avenue." She took out her phone to check the location on the map app. "Holly Hill Apartments."

"Gonna need more than that," Benz stated as she took a gulp of water from a bottle by her seat. "Is it near anything?"

"There's a hotel right next to the complex. There's also a college. Duke University, I think."

"Duke University? That's my dad's alma mater."

"Can he pull some strings?" Jennifer asked hopefully. "Maybe get us some assistance for Randal Solomon? In case we need it?"

"In case we need it?" Benz gave her a puzzled look. "What do you think we're going to do to him?"

"Get the truth out of him, of course. By any means necessary."

"He's not a suspect, Jennifer. He's an old man who's lost his son, daughter-in-law, and grandson."

You are so young. "He also might be aiding my daughter's kidnappers," she said sharply. "At the very least, he might know about the symbols in their attic. If he does, that means he's in league with the thing that took Jacobson. I am *not* taking any chances with him."

—ɯ—

Holly Hill Apartments looked plain, like any other apartment complex Benz had seen. The cars parked in their spaces, the slight cracks in the streets, even the kids playing on the sidewalk, looked like any other street in Durham, North Carolina.

"How'd you find out Stan lived here?"

"During my daughter's trial, the papers did extensive coverage on Stan and his wife," Jennifer answered as she scanned the area for an available parking space. "It helped that Stan was a military hero. The papers treated him like a freaking celebrity."

"Too bad it didn't help him," Benz said as she found a parking space in the back of the complex. "Or his family." *Right near the basketball court!*

"*He* wasn't on trial," Jennifer said in an annoyed voice.

"No, just his child's killer." Benz coasted their car into the first available space and turned off the engine. *A killer I'm helping. Sure as hell didn't think I'd be doing this when I took the badge.*

"Hey, look," Jennifer said, putting a hand on her shoulder. "Just because my daughter's kidnapped doesn't mean I don't feel for the Solomons and what they lost. I'm a parent. I feel for them." She looked at the basketball court directly in front of them. "Especially now."

"But you want to charge into his father's home, demanding answers."

"I'm only doing this to get my daughter back," Jennifer stated in a defensive voice. "Not to add to his pain, whatever that is."

Can I count on you to stay professional? Benz wondered as she searched the older woman's face for a hint of her intentions. She had been easy going enough since leaving Gateway City. On the plane ride to Durham, she had been downright civil. Almost giddy.

But that might go out the window if she met Randal face-to-face.

According to what they had gotten not just from the papers but from the GCPD's database, Randal Solomon lived only a few doors away from where they were parked.

Benz and Jennifer were about to come face-to-face with the man who raised Stan Solomon, maybe even taught him that it was okay to kidnap a cop from her home.

A guilty cop, a voice croaked from the back of her mind. *A guilty, child-killing cop.*

—◆◆◆—

"Benz," Jennifer said, worried that the young detective had lost her nerve. "Are you ready to do this?"

"I was about to ask you the same question," the young detective said, shooting her an exacting glance.

"I'm ready," she answered, glancing out her window.

"I sense a 'but' there."

"Let's just say," Jennifer said, "I know we're not the only ones tracking Stan's father."

Benz gave her a curious side glance. "And how do you know that?"

Fair question, Jennifer thought, turning to face the young detective. "Do you know why Jacobson was taken from his hotel room last night?"

"Because he was looking into Kate's kidnapping and into the Solomons," Benz answered, her eyes searching Jennifer's face as though looking for a hidden agenda. "We agreed on that before we started on this jaunt."

"Yes, but do you know what took him?"

"I had assumed it was Stan or Francine," Benz answered calmly. "But the more I thought about it, the more that didn't make any sense. Neither of them hinted at wanting Jacobson when they took Kate. In fact, they didn't even mention him."

Smart cop, Jennifer thought, nodding her head out of respect. *Why isn't* she *chief of the GCPD?* "That's because ..."—she chanced a looked at the sky—"it wasn't the Solomons that took him."

Benz leaned in close, stern resolve on her young face. "Then who was it?"

"Not who, but *what*."

"Okay, then, *what* was it?"

"A creature," Jennifer answered quietly, afraid someone would hear her. "One that's working on behalf of the Solomons."

Benz's eyes widened, but only slightly. "Are you sure?"

"I saw it," she answered. "With my own eyes. Jacobson saw it too."

—m—

Shit. Benz had to fight to keep her leg from trembling. "What did this ... creature look like?"

"A bat," Jennifer got out before clamping a hand over her mouth, as if expecting to summon the creature just by talking about it. "A giant bat, shaped like a man."

"Wait," Benz cut in, her eyes growing as wide as dinner plates. "A giant bat? There's a giant bat now?!"

"Uh, yes."

"How long have you known about this ... what did you call it?"

"A giant bat, shaped like a man," Jennifer repeated, watching Benz' expression with worried eyes. "I've known about it since it took Kevin."

"Have you ..." Benz took a moment to visualize such a creature. *A freaking man-sized bat, like something out of a comic book.* "Have you seen this creature with your own eyes?"

"Yes," Jennifer answered, wincing either in pain or embarrassment. "We both did."

A bat. Bens bit her bottom lip, her mind constructing an image of it despite her efforts to stop it. A mangy, slimy bat creature, as tall as a man. As tall as a tall man, of course, because why would a monster from another world be short? Complete with hairy large wings, big ears, and fangs the size of steak knives! Benz glanced at her hands, saw them trembling. *Bats. Why'd it have to be a bat? I hate, hate, hate bats!*

"Benz?" Jenifer asked, looking at the detective with concern. "Are you all right?"

Am I all right?! You just told me about a bat creature, now of all times, and you're asking if I'm all right?! "I'm fine," Benz answered quickly. "I just *really* wish you had told me about this before we arrived here."

"Would you have come with me if you did?"

"Not alone, I wouldn't have!" Benz shook her head in disbelief. First supermen and superwomen, and now a bat-man. *Feels like I'm living in a deranged comic book.* "And this … thing saw Jacobson?"

"I told you, Benz, we both saw it," Jennifer answered, nodding. "It even called him, using his girlfriend's phone." She leaned away from Benz, as though she were about to explode.

Which wasn't that far from the truth.

This thing can talk too?! And use a phone?! Benz balled her hands into fists to keep from screaming. *What else can this thing do?!* She shot Jennifer a strained look. *And why the hell didn't you tell me, or Isenguard, before we left Gateway City without backup?!* Benz swallowed; her throat was suddenly as dry as the Sahara. *She mentioned Jacobson' girlfriend.* Benz remembered an attractive redhead at the precinct's Christmas Party, hanging proudly off Jacobson's arm. *Joan. Joan Collins.* "How's Jacobson's girlfriend involved in this?"

"The thing got her phone, somehow," Jennifer answered in a hushed whisper. "It tossed it to Jacobson before taking off into the sky."

"Taking off? It can fly, too?"

"On leathery bat wings. And I wouldn't be surprised if it's following us right now."

"Because it took Jacobson," Benz reasoned. "I get it." She let out an exasperated sigh. "Really wish you'd told me all this before I agreed to come with you."

"Why? So you could back out?"

"So I could request backup. If what you're saying about this thing's true, we're not going to be able to fight it on our own." *Should've taken Isenguard with us.*

"I hope it won't come to that," Jennifer said.

"If that was true, you wouldn't have told me about it right now."

"Noted," she said quietly. "So what do you want to do?"

"Keep with the plan," Benz said, blowing a strand of hair from her face. "It's all we can do for now. But we see anything strange in the sky, we request backup from local law enforcement."

"Sounds good," Jennifer agreed, opening her passenger door. "Let's get going while we still have daylight."

"Yeah, let's."

"Here it is," Jennifer whispered as they stood outside a tan-colored door labeled 31A. "Randal Solomon's apartment."

"Well, let's give it a knock," Benz said, moving to rap her fingers on the door.

"No! Wait!" Jennifer hissed, grabbing her hand. "We don't know what he'll do!"

"We came here to talk to him," the detective insisted. "If we're going to get your daughter, and Jacobson, back, we have to interview him."

"I know, it's just …" Jennifer paused, indecision in her eyes. She had been hunting the Solomons for so long, that they were like monsters to her. If she spoke to their father, she'd see them as people. He *would* make her see them as people.

She wasn't ready for that.

It might distract her from bringing Kate home.

She couldn't let anything keep that from happening. She had come too far!

"I know you're used to demonizing the Solomons." Benz rested both of her hands on the older woman's shoulders, fixing her with a stern look. "But if you want to see Kate again, you're going to have to let that go. Can you?"

"You're right," Jennifer admitted under her breath. "Let's do it." She turned to the door. "Let's give it a knock—"

The door swung open quickly, revealing the barrel of a shotgun.

—⟋⟍—

Shit. Benz raised her hands instinctively. "We're not here to fight."

"Yeah, I'll bet," Randal Solomon growled, aiming his shotgun at the two women. "I'll bet that's the same thing your Gestapo girl told my grandson."

He was barely over five feet six, with a heavy build and silvery hair. A curiously black mustache decorated his sneering lips. He looked as much like an older Stan Solomon, as Jennifer looked like an older Kate Barrow.

"Mr. Solomon, I'm Detective Julie Benz," she started. "I'm here to talk to you about—"

"My son," Randal cut her off, "as if I know anything."

"Please," Jennifer cut in, her tone thick with desperation, "I just want my daughter back!"

Randal seemed to growl as he turned to her. "Your daughter?" Then it seemingly hit him. "So *you're* the bitch that raised the bitch that shot my grandson!"

"I … I …" Jennifer blubbered.

"If you think, for a second, that I'm gonna help you, after what your 'daughter' did to my family…"

What did he just call her? "Mr. Solomon," Benz said after finding her voice, "we just want to talk."

"Right," he chuckled humorlessly. "Because that's what you're known for! Why the hell would I help you?"

Think fast, Julie. "Because I'll bet you're as torn up about what your son and daughter-in-law have done as we are," Benz answered after seeing pictures of a younger Stan, and possibly siblings, decorating the wall behind him. "And more, I'll bet you want them back as much as Mrs. Barrow wants her daughter."

"Show me your badge," Randal growled, "nice and easy."

In full view of his watchful eyes, Benz reached into her jacket pocket and pulled her badge out for him to see. "Now, can we please come in?"

"You're not going to leave until you do, are you?"

"Please!" Jennifer piped up. "He has my daughter! Your son has my daughter!"

"Keep her quiet and you can come in." Randal glowered at Jennifer as though she were an annoying insect. "But get one thing straight. You're not in control here." He lowered his gun. "I think for a second you're up to something, you're getting out of my house."

—⚶—

He almost shot us! Jennifer swallowed nervously, staring at Stan's father as he sat in an easy chair facing them. He kept his gun in his lap and a glass of liquor in his hand, looking like he couldn't care less if they liked it or not.

That Benz was a cop seemed to mean nothing to him.

No wonder his son grew up to be a kidnapper!

"Talk," he barked angrily. "Now."

"Has Stan been in contact with you?" Benz asked, balancing herself on one of two rickety chairs Randal had motioned for her to sit in.

Jennifer sat in the other one, knowing a power move when she saw one. As long as Randal was comfortable and they weren't, he felt he controlled the conversation. She and James did the same thing when they argued.

"No," he answered casually.

"What about Francine Solomon?"

"Nope."

"Has anyone associated with them tried to contact you?" Benz continued, holding a notepad in her hands. She had managed, through her nervousness, to write things down. How, Jennifer had *no* idea.

"No." Randal took a sip of his drink, a finger of bourbon. Or was it whiskey?

"Mr. Solomon, we need you to—"

"Why did your daughter kill my grandson?"

Jennifer jumped at how abruptly he changed tactics. One second, he was looking at Benz. The next, he was looking at her. "I don't know," she answered hoarsely. *Why am I letting this man scare me?* "I assume it was in the line of duty."

"Or maybe because you and your husband taught her it was okay to kill black kids."

"How dare you!" Jennifer started, jumping to her feet. "I raised my daughter to be a good person!"

"When kids act like monsters, it's usually the parent's fault," Randal declared, glaring at Jennifer like an angry rottweiler would at a cat, or an intruder. "So I'm asking you, why'd you raise your bitch of a daughter to be a monster?"

"I didn't raise Kate to be … what you're saying she is!" Jennifer continued, her face growing beet red. "Your grandson got in her way! Who does that?!"

"Who chases a perp, hopped up on drugs, into someone's backyard?!" Randal asked in a voice as cold as the grave. "What empty-headed dumbass fires their gun without checking who or what they're firing at?!"

"That's not how it happened, damn you!"

"Oh, that's right! Because you were there!"

"Everyone, stop!" Benz snapped, ending the argument before it got farther. She turned to Randal. "Mr. Solomon, I know you have no love for us—"

"Not even a *little*," he got out in a savage growl.

"But do you know what your kids are doing in Gateway City?"

"I haven't spoken to my son or his wife since I put my grandson in the ground," came the icy reply as he leaned back in his chair. "So why don't you tell me?"

—⁂—

Since you asked … Benz licked her lips, staring Randal in his cold eyes. "My people think that Stan and Francine are enacting a purge."

"Of what?"

153

"Police officers," she answered, a grave look on her face. "What they did to Kate, they're doing to other members of law enforcement."

"Anything these fine men and women have in common?" Randal asked in a flippant voice. "Besides being cops?"

"A history of brutality and corruption," Benz answered, eyeing the comfortable way he handled the gun in his lap. "Some even have cases that go to trial—"

"But let me guess," Randal interrupted, his lip drawn back in a sneer, "they're either thrown out or acquitted."

He's enjoying this. "Yes."

"Seems my kids are doing what you guys should've done years ago."

Your kids. "But unlike Kate Barrow, the Solomons are bringing these officers back," Benz stated. "They're either taken from their homes or off the street, only to turn up days later, completely shellshocked."

"Got a scare, eh?"

"Yes," Benz agreed, nodding her head. "After that, they put in for early retirement."

"Heh," Randal chuckled mirthlessly. "My heart bleeds."

"And guess what? Days later, they come down with deep psychological problems. Psychotic breaks, nervous breakdowns, whatever you want to call it. As if the Solomons broke their minds."

"Wish I could say I'm sorry to hear that."

You have to feel something! "The lucky ones get counseling," Benz continued. "The not-so-lucky ones? They're either committed or commit suicide."

Randal fidgeted in his seat but didn't break eye contact. "That it?"

"If the Solomons could do that to seasoned cops, think of what they could do to other people."

"Other people?

"A campaign like this won't stop with just one group," Benz explained in a grim voice. "They'll target others. They'll grow bolder and bolder, until they hurt the wrong person."

"And?"

"And then … who knows?" Benz fixed him with a penetrating stare "But do you really want to live in a world that would create?"

"Look, Detective—"

"Would Brian?"

Randal hissed, her words hitting a soft spot. "Well Brian *won't* be doing that, so I have nothing to lose." He motioned to the door. "I've listened to your concerns. Now get out of my house."

—m—

No! It can't end here! "There's something else!" Jennifer blurted out, her head shaking as though it were about to explode.

"There always is," Randal grumbled, turning his eyes on her.

"The Solomons aren't the only superpowered people in Gateway City!" *Still can't believe I have to say that with a straight face!* "Something else followed them. Maybe even works for them!"

Randal paused, mid-drink. "What?"

"It's large," Jennifer continued. "Muscular too, and intelligent. It's cleaning up after the Solomons, tying up loose ends! For God's sake, it burned down their house a few nights ago, just to destroy these!" She tossed the file of Jacobson's pictures at Randal's lap.

It landed atop his legs in one toss. "What are—"

"Please, Mr. Solomon," Jennifer begged, clasping her hands together as if in prayer. "I know you feel my little girl deserves what happened to her! Believe me, I can relate!"

"Can you?" Randal's grip on his glass tightened so hard she could see it, straining against the pressure. "Can you *really?*"

"The day Brian died—"

"Was killed," Randal corrected venomously.

"We *both* lost our kids." Tears ran down Jennifer's face as she imagined, not for the first time, what horrors Katie was enduring. "I'm not trying to trivialize your pain. I can't. I'm just trying to get my little girl back."

Randal glared at her, but it wasn't as intense as before. His lips turned up in a sneer as he looked at the file in his lap. "Lady, you got some nerve pulling on that string."

"Please, help me, and together we can save both of our children," Jennifer declared, "and make sure what happened to Brian will never happen to anyone else. Ever again."

155

—⁕—

There's the pitch, Benz thought as she watched Randal for a reaction. *Let's see if he takes it.* There was an intensity to the man. She had to wonder how Stan grew up with it.

And how it affected him.

Randal Solomon let out a weary sigh, the wall coming down from his face. "I told Stan to be careful."

"Careful?"

"About people like *you*," he said, stabbing a finger at Benz. "Cops. Lawmakers. People who say they're 'here to help.' It's been my experience that they never help people like us." He pointed at his black skin; in case the meaning of his comment was lost. "People like you hit us with firehoses, beat us with nightsticks, sic dogs on us, because we're fighting for our rights."

"That was over forty years ago," Benz declared solemnly.

"Yeah, and you know what? Nothing changes," Randal declared. "Society never changes. It just likes saying it does." He picked up something from beside his easy chair, held it in meaty fingers. "Everyone likes to think the past is past, but then something comes along that brings it right back to the present."

Benz saw it was a framed picture of a young boy sitting happily on a park bench. A young biracial boy of about eight or nine. "Let me guess, Brian?"

"This was the last time I saw him," Randal declared, his eyes on the photo. Brian had an ice cream cone in his hands, vanilla ice cream streaming between his little fingers. Next to him sat Stan to his left and Randal to his right.

They held matching ice cream cones.

"Surprise visit," Randal explained proudly. "Before Stan shipped out for another tour. Francine took the picture. I asked her to be in it, but she bowed out."

"She sounds nice." *Would've loved to have met her then.*

"She was," Randal agreed, nodding his head. "Said she had all the time in the world to be with Brian. I only had a little. So I needed to enjoy it. To genuinely enjoy it." Randal gently put the picture back by his chair. "She was so right."

—⚉—

"Least in that, we agree." Jennifer took a small picture out of her wallet and handed it to Randal. It was a picture of Kate back when she was eight or nine. She sat on a swing, a large grin plastered on her face. Her knees were bruised because she had fallen off it earlier.

"I told her she didn't need to go on the swing again," Jennifer found herself saying as Randal turned the picture over. "But my little girl refused. Said she had to master it. No matter what. Or how long it took."

"Funny what kids say"—Randal swallowed, a wistful smile on his face—"to make us proud."

"I know," Jennifer agreed, nodding her head slowly, "Mr. Solomon."

"You've been in my house long enough. Call me Randal."

"Thank you, Randal," Jennifer said, happy she had reached him. "I'm sorry my little girl took Brian from you. Can you please help me get her back?"

The old man sighed, gazing at Kate's childhood picture. He picked up Brian's picture, held it next to hers. "I'll try, Mrs.—"

"Jennifer," she corrected gently. "Call me Jennifer."

"I'll try ... Jennifer," Randal said, his lips trying out the feel of her name. He glanced at the file in his lap. "But I can't promise much."

"I'll take what I can get," came the hopeful reply. "And thank you."

—⚉—

The kinship of parents. Benz looked away to wipe off a tear that snuck past her eyelids. *Strongest thing I've ever seen.*

Strong enough to make or break a case.

"This other ... superpowered person," Randal said as he handed Jennifer her picture while putting his away, "you say it destroyed Stan and Francine's house?"

"Yes." *Really wish she'd told me about it before we left Gateway City.* "According to Mrs. Barrow," Benz said, "it took Officer Kevin Jacobson too."

"Jacobson," Randal said, a faraway look in his eyes. "Wait, he was there when Brian was killed!"

"He was Officer Barrow's senior partner," Benz said, shooting Jennifer a worried glance. The last thing they needed was for Randal to undo the understanding they had reached.

"This thing happen to look like a bat? Like a human-sized bat?"

"Yes!" Jennifer shouted, her eyes seemingly bulging out of her head. "You've seen it!"

"No," Randal answered reluctantly. "But I've heard of it." He opened the file, seeing the images of the symbols scrawled all over the Solomons' attic. "Dammit, Francine, what have you done?"

—⚶—

Dammit, Francine?! Jennifer's eyes widened at the apprehension on Randal's face. *She's done something* else *bad? What other bad thing could she possibly have done?!*

"What do you mean?" Benz asked, fixing on Randal's words before he, or Jennifer, forgot them.

Thank God for Benz, she thought as she watched Randal mull over her question. *Asking the questions I'm too afraid to ask. Knew there was a reason I brought her along.*

"I was hoping she hadn't called them," Randal answered, staring at the symbols in the photos. "Hoping against hope, even when I read about what they'd done. The abilities they showed, I hoped she hadn't dragged my boy into her madness. But after what you just told me, I gotta face the truth."

He's not affected by the symbols, Jennifer realized, not seeing a speck of blood drip from Randal's nose. *Doesn't even have a headache. He's seen them before. But when?* She was on pins and needles, afraid to say the wrong thing and ruin the truce she and Randal had made.

But she also had to know more.

"Hadn't called whom?" Benz asked confidently, arching her brow at the older man.

Thank God for Benz, Jennifer thought again as Randal mulled the question over.

"I shouldn't even say their names," he mumbled, more to himself than to the two women sitting in front of him.

"If you're worried about harassment, don't be," Benz stated, putting a calming hand on Randal's knee, which was shaking. "You don't have to worry about anything from the GCPD. They don't even know we're here."

"Young lady, the last thing I'm worried about is harassment from *you* guys."

I have to speak. "Please, Randal," Jennifer said, putting her hand on his other knee. *We probably look ridiculous.* "Tell us who 'they' are. And why Francine would call them."

An eye on a nearby window, Randal motioned for them to come closer. "What do you know of Francine's family?"

"That she comes from an Irish background," Benz answered. "From her father's side."

"That's true, but not entirely. Her mother's side is from South Africa," he said. "They're called Afrikaners, descendants of the Dutch that arrived in the seventeenth and eighteenth centuries."

"I didn't know that," Jennifer said, blinking in surprise. *The things I've learned on this journey so far could fill a stack of books!*

"Most folks don't, something else edited from history class," Randal said in a voice touched with bitter knowledge. "One of the reasons I can't stand public schools. Francine still has family on that side. Including an aunt that no one talks to."

"No one? Who is she?"

"Her name is, get this, Athena."

"After the Greek goddess of wisdom?"

"So you know that," Randal said, seemingly looking at Jennifer in a new light. "That's good, and a little surprising."

"I know a few things," she said proudly.

"Continue with the story please," Benz cut in. "But first, could we get something to drink? I'm feeling a little parched."

159

—⚊—

This is better, Benz thought as she sat in a chair in Randal's study in the back of his apartment. *Much better.* The chair she sat in was plush, like his easy chair in the living room.

Jennifer lounged on a sofa in the corner, drinking coffee. She looked sleepy, her eyelids drooping as she looked at the rest of room.

Awards decorated the walls, as did stacks of books and other memorabilia that flanked the massive wooden desk that was Randal's workspace.

"Hell of a life," Benz commented, taking a swig of water.

"This used to be Stan's room, back when he was a kid," he said over his shoulder. "Once he moved out, my wife and me turned this to a workout room. Then, when she … passed, I had no one to work out for. Especially when Stan stopped talking to me after he joined the military. So I turned it into a study. It serves me well."

Wondered why this place lacked a woman's touch, Benz thought snidely. *Talk about loss.* First his wife, then his son, and, finally, his grandson. No wonder he had retreated from society. *Bet my next paycheck Francine's the one that coaxed him out of his shell.*

"This is where I do the heavy thinking," Randal said, snapping Benz out of her thoughts. "Now, about that aunt of Francine's …"

"Yeah?"

"She's the black sheep of the family. And that's from a *family* of black sheep."

"When Francine took Kate," Benz said as she sat next to him at his desk, "she said her family doesn't talk to her. Hasn't since she married Stan."

"They all cut ties with her, bunch of assholes. Francine and Stan have been married for twenty years, and I *still* haven't met them. They never even got to meet Brian."

"And yet, this Aunt Athena …?"

"Was the only one who kept in contact with her," Randal revealed. "They were thick as thieves, even when Francine was a kid. Her parents tried to keep them apart. From what Francine told me, they were ashamed of her."

"Athena or Francine?"

"Heh, who knows?"

Benz looked over her shoulder, saw Jennifer dozing on the couch. Even in sleep, she had a troubled look on her face. Just like she did on the flight from Gateway City. *Nightmares. Probably been having them since Kate was taken.* She looked back to Randal. *Hope I can put them to rest.*

"So why are you doing this?"

"Excuse me?"

"I get why she's here," Randal jabbed a finger at Jennifer. "But this is way over the line for you. Way out of your jurisdiction too. So what's up?"

Should've known we'd cross this bridge. Benz sighed, the weight of regret planting her in her chair. She massaged her neck as Randal waited, reluctant to tell him anything.

"Well? I'm waiting."

"I'm just trying to right a wrong," she answered, turning away from his piercing gaze. "And put this craziness to rest before it gets worse."

"Uh-huh," Randal grunted. "Right."

—※—

Jennifer found herself sitting on a foldout chair on a bright, sunny day. *What?* She looked around, confused. *I was in ...* "Where are we—"

"Shhhh," James said quietly, putting a finger to his lips. He looked so good in his Ascot clothes, his hair perfectly slicked back. "It's starting, honey."

"Starting?" Jennifer blinked in surprise, seeing that she was dressed in the red dress she wore when they went to church. She even wore her pearl necklace. *Haven't worn this since ...* A bell snapped her attention to a stage. *Kate's graduation!*

The local sheriff stood at a podium, graduates at his right. Garbed in full police uniform, they looked out onto the crowd. They tried to look authoritative, but for the relatives who came to see them, they looked like fresh-faced kids.

Kate, especially.

She stood in the first row in her police regalia, looking ready to uphold the law.

I'm … here? Jennifer wondered, blinking back her confusion. *How'd I …*

"It's a privilege to be asked to speak at your commencement ceremony today," the sheriff started, "and I thank you for this prized opportunity."

"No!" Jennifer desperately ran for the stage. *It's not too late! I can stop this!*

"Do not tarnish what you have accomplished here by losing sight of who you are when you don your uniform …"

"Kate!" Jennifer screamed, waiving her arms to get her daughter's attention. "Katie!"

"What you have chosen to do is a mission—a calling, no less, to be guardians of the public safety …"

Yes! Embers of hope sparked as Kate turned to face her. *That's right, baby! Look at Momma!*

"Do not take the tasks inherent in this noble and distinguished undertaking lightly," the sheriff intoned, his voice deepening with every word.

I'll keep you from Gateway City! Jennifer reached the stairs of the stage, took them two at a time. *I'll make sure you never meet the Solomons! That's a mother's job! That's my job!*

"Where you will help old ladies across the street …"

Almost there!

"You will save lives …"

There! Jennifer reached the stage, grabbed Kate's arm. "We're going—"

"And you will take lives too."

She's not moving! Jennifer pulled with all her might, but her daughter might as well have been frozen on the stage. *Why isn't she moving?!* "James, help me!"

"You will gun down black kids in the streets," the sheriff continued without missing a beat. "Gleefully filling their bodies with bullets …"

"Help me!" She turned to the audience, eyes bulging out of her head. "Help me!"

"And your loved ones will look on, knowing they're responsible …"

"Please!"

"And I will have to clean up the mess."

Jennifer turned slowly, the hair on the back of her neck standing on end.

Standing at the podium, in place of the sheriff, was the Solomons' batlike enforcer. Sporting a powerful, muscular frame, its ivory-colored skin sparkled as sunlight turned to moonlight, and day to night.

"No," she stammered, backing away from the horrible sight. "No."

"I told you to stay away." Reptilian lips drew back into a rictus grin as the creature cracked human-looking knuckles. "I thought taking your pet cop would be message enough."

"H-h-help." Shaking like a leaf, Jennifer turned to the audience for help, barely getting her voice above a whisper. "Help ..."

"But I guess I'll have to take a little more."

Hooked claws dug into Jennifer's throat before she had time to scream.

—⚊—

Oh, come on! Benz nearly jumped out of her skin as Jennifer screamed, clawing at the air. Benz grabbed her by the shoulders, shaking her as hard as she could without hurting her. "Wake up, Jennifer! Wake up!"

Randal stumbled into the room, wearing only a bathrobe and slippers. "What the hell's going on?!"

"She's having a nightmare!" Benz shouted, still shaking Jennifer. "I'm trying to shake her out of it!"

"Let me try," he said, quickly pushing her aside. "I got a knack!"

What's he going to do? "What can you—"

"Trust me," Randal said before slapping Jennifer hard across the face. "I'm a parent!"

"Ow!" Jennifer snapped out of her frenzy, gawking first at Randal, then at Benz. "What happened?!"

Not liking his approach! "You were having a nightmare," Benz answered, switching places with Randal while flashing him a dirty look. "Damn near woke up the neighbors!"

As if on cue, harsh pounding snapped their necks to the living room.

"Shit." Randal waddled to the living room. "I'm already in hot water because jackasses keep coming here!"

Hope he can handle them. Benz gazed at Jennifer; a concerned look plastered on her face. "Are you all right?"

"I'm fine," she said, taking quick, heavy breaths. "I … I just need a minute!"

"Me too, Jennifer." Benz sat in a chair next to her, willing her heart to slow down. "Me too."

—⁘—

Can't believe I screamed like that. Jennifer's cheeks burned with raw embarrassment as Randal entered the study.

"Everyone here okay?" he asked, looking first at Benz.

"We're fine."

"And you?" He shot Jennifer an annoyed look. "Ready to act like an adult now?"

Son of a … "I'm fine."

"So what was that?"

"I just had a nightmare," Jennifer answered quietly.

"Uh-huh." Randal looked her up and down. "Care to share it with us?"

"She doesn't have to do that," Benz said, putting a protective hand on Jennifer's shoulder.

"The hell she doesn't," Randal snapped. "Screams like a damn banshee, wakes me and the neighbors out of a dead sleep, and she doesn't get to explain herself?"

Night? Jennifer's eyes flicked to a clock on the wall. *Good lord, it's nine!* "How long have we been here?"

"Six hours," Benz answered, a concerned look on her face.

"How could you let me sleep that long?! The longer we take, the harder it's gonna be to get Kate back!"

"You needed the sleep," she answered sternly. "You've been looking like death warmed over since I met you."

"I'll sleep when we get Kate back," Jennifer declared in a desperate voice.

"You wanna find her?" Randal cut in; his brown eyes blazing. "Then be in proper condition. Because what we're gonna do, you'll need all the strength you can muster. And you get that from proper sleep!"

"I ...," Jennifer chirped, so taken aback by his words that she couldn't mount a defense.

"You wanted this, lady," Randal continued before Benz could intercede. "*You* started down this path! You want us to follow you? Then treat us with respect and tell us what's going on!" He snatched a chair from his desk, looking too angry to notice how awkward his movements were. "Now tell us everything!" He planted his butt in the chair, glaring at her with accusing eyes. "Now!"

—⚊⚊

Once again, not my approach, Benz thought as she turned from Randal to Jennifer. *God help us if this gets women to open up.*

"I had a nightmare," Jennifer said in a quite murmur. "About the bat-man."

Of course *she responds to harsh treatment!* Benz mentally threw up her hands. *No wonder Kate shot Brian Solomon the way she did! Look who she has for a role model!*

"The bat-man," Randal said, shaking his head. "That's what you're calling it, eh?"

"It walks like a man and looks like a giant bat," Jennifer said icily. "What would *you* call it?"

"Yaksha," he answered, looking as if he'd eaten something sour, "of the Yakshini."

"You know its name?" Benz gave him an aghast look. "You've known, this whole time?"

"Since the minute I saw my son and daughter-in-law in the papers, and reports of what they'd done," Randal answered, giving her a casual look. "They couldn't have gotten their ... superpowers without him."

"He's real?" *Dumb question, Benz!* "How do you know about him?"

165

"Remember Francine's aunt?" Randal chuckled without mirth. "She told me about him."

"Is Yaksha his real name?"

"It's what she called him," Randal answered, sitting back in his chair.

"And what is he to the Solomons?" Benz asked, her voiced touched with impatience.

"He's their go-between," Randal answered after letting out a long sigh.

Between who, dammit?! "Between who?"

"Them and their benefactors," Randal answered. "The ones that gave them their powers. And their marching orders."

Their marching orders. Benz shivered while Jennifer stared at Randal in mystified stupor. *Everything they're doing in Gateway City's at the bidding of someone else! But who? For what purpose? And for how long?*

— ∞ —

I knew coming here was the right idea," Jennifer thought with relief. The fact that Randal knew this … bat thing by name meant she was on the right track. "How'd the Solomons even contact something like that?"

"Francine probably remembers some rituals from talking to her aunt," Randal answered. "Like I said, they were thick as thieves when she was a little girl. The things her aunt told her, she never forgot. She even told them to me when she would come to see me."

"Why would she come to see you?"

"Because she loved me as her father-in-law? Hell, she loved me more than her biological father."

Right. Racist. Remember that, Jennifer! "And who are these … interdimensional beings the Solomons contacted?"

"She calls them the Arbiters."

That's … amazingly on-the-nose, Jennifer thought, blinking in surprise. "You'd think they'd have a name that's more … exotic."

"You and me too," Randal agreed. "And I'm sure they do, but Francine was making it easy for me to understand. Her aunt called them something else. Something I'm not going to say. We do *not* want to call those guys."

"But we need them to get Kate back," Jennifer screeched. "We need them!"

"We don't need them for that. I'm telling you about them to give you context for Yaksha. When the Arbiters give people their powers, he's part of the package."

Something tells me those powers aren't free, Jennifer thought darkly. "And in return?"

"They have to say goodbye to their old lives," Randal answered in a solemn voice. "And everyone that's part of them."

"That means you," Benz said, cutting in at last. "And the rest of your family. Is that the reason you haven't tried to contact them after they took Kate Barrow?"

"Honestly," Randal answered, his face exuding sadness, "I'd hoped it was fake news. Crap made to make my son and his wife look bad." He fixed Benz with an accusing look. "That happens, especially when people want to ignore their complicity in tragedy."

"Easy, Mr. Solomon," she said, not avoiding his gaze. "We're not going to get anywhere by pointing fingers."

"It's funny how people never want to point fingers during a tragedy when they have to take responsibility."

Get him back on track! "There was a police officer," Jennifer blurted out quickly. "Officer Kevin Jacobson. He was helping me find Kate. We saw this Yaksha on the rooftop of a building across from his apartment."

"Okay?" Randal gestured for her to continue.

"He also saw it at the Solomons' house," Jennifer continued. "It tossed him out a window before burning the house down!"

"Damn. I really liked that house."

Is that all he has to say? "You don't sound the least bit surprised."

"It fits his pattern," Randal said, leaning back in his chair to knuckle his eyes. "Yaksha's job is to close the book on their candidates' old lives so they commit to their new ones."

"Consisting of what?" Jennifer had drawn her knees to her chest, afraid for her feet to touch the floor. She gazed at Stan's father with rapt attention, afraid to speak above a whisper, in case this Yaksha was listening.

And after her nightmare about Kate, she was sure it was.

—⚏—

"So it's covering their tracks," Benz reasoned, worried at seeing Jennifer so hypnotized by Randal's words. "The house. Kate's partner. Even Jennifer's dreams. It's trying to warn people away. To intimidate them."

"Like a leg breaker for the mob," Randal agreed, snapping his fingers. "Now you got it."

A demonic leg breaker. Benz let out a weary sigh, feeling like a lifeboat adrift in unfamiliar seas. "So to get Kate back, we're going to have to talk to this Yaksha." *That might as well happen!*

"We should talk to Francine's aunt, first," Jennifer countered.

"Gonna be hard," Randal said, shaking his head, "on account of her being dead."

"What? Are you serious?"

"Yup. She died a couple of months ago."

Damn. Benz's lips turned up in a scowl. *We missed her by weeks.* "Then how are we going to get this Yaksha to talk to us?"

"Oh, we're not." Randal raised a cautionary finger. "We're gonna talk to my son."

"That's a relief."

"But Francine will come when we do," he added, a grave look on his face. "And so will Yaksha."

A small whining sound escaped Jennifer's lips, making Benz put a protective arm around her. "Are you sure?"

"Francine's fiercely loyal to Stan. And Yaksha's loyal to both of them."

He's so matter-of-fact about all this. Jennifer's whining sounds grew worse, making Benz put another arm around her. "And I take it you know how to get Stan to talk to us."

"I'm his father," Randal answered, puffing up his chest. "Of course I do."

—❧—

"Then do it now!" Jennifer almost sprung out of Benz's embrace like a coiled spring. "We have to do it now!"

"We do it tomorrow." Randal calmly pulled away from her. "It's gonna take a lot of work, and we're gonna need our strength." He got up from his seat, a smug look on his face. "In the meantime, get some sleep. Preferably in a hotel." He pointed at the door leading out of his study. "We got one, next door."

"We have to call Stan now!" Jennifer's hands were like claws on Randal's shoulder. "Kate can't last much longer! I can feel it! Please! We have to call Stan now!"

Randal looked down his nose at her as if she were crazy.

Jennifer beseeched the older man with her eyes with such fervor that she barely felt Benz's arms pulling her back.

"Jennifer," Benz said, cocking her head at the exit. "We should go."

"But—!"

"We got what we need." Her stern face was all Jennifer could see. "More than we thought we'd get. Let's go while we can."

"I …" Kate's agonized face danced with Yaksha's, like a ghost, before Jennifer's eyes. "Fine."

They left the apartment, Benz taking up the rear in case Jennifer tried to grab Randal again. She almost thought she heard him chuckle as they stepped into the cold night.

—❧—

Dammit, Kate, your mother is killing me, Benz thought as they drove to the hotel Randal told them about. It wasn't exactly next door. There was a long, winding road to travel.

Benz gave Jennifer furtive glances, as if expecting her to jump out of her passenger seat and run back to Randal's home. *First Stan and Francine's enhancement, and now we have to worry about a demonic enforcer? Where will it end?*

And how'd all this happen without the GCPD, or anyone, knowing about it?!

169

Benz checked her rearview mirror, relieved there were no cars behind them. "You wanna talk about your little outburst?" *I'd sure like to!*

"I'm sorry," Jennifer mumbled.

"Didn't catch that."

"I'm sorry," she repeated a little louder.

"Do I have to worry about you?" *God, I'm sounding like Frank now!*

"No, you—"

"Think, before you answer."

Her statement was met with silence, which, hopefully, meant Jennifer was actually thinking.

"I just want my little girl back," she finally answered.

"I get that, but this is even bigger than her now," Benz said as she checked her rearview mirror again.

"Not to me."

"That tunnel vision's what got all of us in this mess."

"Oh, not you too," Jennifer started, looking at Benz aghast. "Don't tell me you agree with what the Solomons did!"

"I don't," Benz said calmly, not even meeting the older woman's cold stare. "But I'm not going to put Kate on a pedestal either. And trust me, no one at the station is doing so."

"They're just jealous of her."

"Or maybe they know her better than you do," Benz reasoned. "From what I've learned, you hadn't talked to Kate in over two years. For someone that loves their child, that's a hell of a long time to go dark."

"From what you learned?" Jennifer gawked at Benz, her mouth agape in shock. "What is *that* supposed to mean?!"

"That I asked around before talking to you," Benz said, keeping her voice measured and calm. "It's called doing research."

—⚹—

Knew I'd have to answer for this, Jennifer thought as she digested Benz's words, *one day*. "I *do* love my daughter."

"Never doubted that."

You sure? "But that doesn't mean I agreed with her decision."

"In regard to what? Being a cop?"

170

Seems you got all the answers. Jennifer actually missed Jacobson. He never asked questions about her past. Never lost focus. But he was gone, and Benz was all she had. So Jennifer had to work with her. "I never wanted her to be a cop. Especially as a woman."

"Little sexist, there?"

"No, just protective. Look, the world demands more from us than it does from men," Jennifer explained in a haughty voice. "Especially in an occupation like this. The military, medical, and service industries, they chew us up and spit us out. You know it. I know it. And Kate knew it."

"And that's why you stopped talking to her the minute she went off to police academy," Benz said.

"She could've been anything else! Anywhere else! She could've found a job that respected her! Kept her safe and comfortable!" Jennifer's nose flared as she remembered the shouting matches between her and Kate after she was accepted into the police academy. *God, the horrible things we said to each other!* Jennifer winced, placing a hand on her heart. *Malignant, hateful things.* She swallowed down a wave of regret. *I actually wanted her to fail!*

"Jennifer?" Benz asked, giving her an expectant look.

"But no," she continued, Benz's words getting her revved up all over again. "That wasn't enough for her! And now she's paying for it!"

"And it's up to you to clean up after her, right?"

Whoa. Jennifer blinked, not expecting the comeback. "In a manner, yes."

"Uh-huh," Benz snorted, checking her rearview mirror again.

"Don't you judge me! You don't know what it's like to have a child!"

"No, I know what it's like for a parent to project their fears onto one," Benz said coolly. "Selfish as that is."

Did she just call me selfish?! Jennifer was about to give Benz a piece of her mind when the detective's eyes widened at what she saw in her rearview mirror. "What's—"

Then something collided with their car, knocking them off the road!

—⚍—

The rental car rolled over and over, dashing Benz and Jennifer about, before coming to rest on its top in a forest clearing.

Jesus, Benz thought, her ears ringing. *What hit—* Then she remembered Randal's stories. *Yaksha!* "Jennifer? You all right?" She turned to see the beleaguered mother out cold, hanging upside down from her seat.

Least she kept her seat belt on. Benz unbuckled hers, falling to the car's ceiling. Knives of pain shot up from her shoulder, almost making her black out. Gritting her teeth, she unbuckled Jennifer's seatbelt.

Her body hit with a dull thud.

He's gonna come back. Benz pulled her gun from its holster. *Have to get away from here.* She glanced at Jennifer. *No. Get away from her. Give her time to escape.*

Painfully, she pulled herself out of the downed car. When she was free of the wreck, she went into a crouch, her gun up and ready to fire. *Where is he?*

Benz glanced back at the car, surprised it wasn't totaled. If she could get it back on its wheels, maybe it could still drive! "Jennifer?"

She didn't answer.

"Jennifer!" Benz saw she was still knocked out. *Dammit!*

Blood streamed from a nasty cut on Jennifer's forehead, and her left arm was pinned at an odd angle.

Benz was about to reach for her when she heard the flapping of wings. "Where are you?!"

"Right here."

Something huge landed on the car's undercarriage, making Benz whip her gun up at the sound. What she saw blew away any common sense she had left.

A towering figure sat crouched above her. It's skin was white as porcelain, reflecting the moonlight. Folded batlike wings adorned impossibly broad shoulders. Its head was square—too square to be made by natural means. Sharp points jutted out the back, giving the impression of bat ears.

He stared at her, amusement shining from eyes as black as coal. Rubbery lips curled into a smile, showing rows of sharp teeth. "You're Benz."

"I am," came the wary answer.

"Nice to meet you."

It knows my name. Benz wasn't surprised, and that scared her more than the creature, because it meant she was growing accustomed to this craziness. "How do you know my name?"

"We know you."

We? Benz facepalmed mentally, pursing her lips in frustration. *Oh, of course there's a "we" somewhere!* "Let us go?"

"You? Yes." Yaksha's head tilted down, as if he knew Jennifer lay in the car. "Her? No."

"How'd you find us?"

"Take a wild guess."

Does he know we've been talking to Randal? Benz wondered, arching her brow while staring at the creature. *Are the two of them working together?* Randal did seem very eager to get her and Jennifer out of his house.

Randal had already admitted, rather nonchalantly, to having knowledge of Stan and Francine's transformation. And it was clear he had no love for Kate Barrow, or anyone connected to her.

But was it enough to aid the creature protecting them?

"I'm not leaving without her," Benz stated firmly.

"Well now," Yaksha said, shrugging his broad shoulders. "Then you're not leaving."

Wha ... Jennifer was half awake when her eyes fluttered open. But the guttural alien voice, snarling threats above, slapped her back to the world with a rough hand. *What happened?*

Twisted metal surrounded her and what used to be their car.

They were driving, and then ...

We had a wreck. Her mind worked at half speed putting the details together. *No ... Something hit us ...* She bit back a scream as pain lit up

173

her arm. *Turned us over.* Blood dribbled down her face. *I got cut.* Her eyes grew wide. *Benz! Where's Benz?!*

Gritting her teeth against waves of nausea that threatened to drown her, she turned to the driver seat. *Where is she?*

The car shook, as though something were on top of it.

Sitting. Waiting. Listening?

The source of the voice!

Oh dear lord … Jennifer clamped her one good hand over her mouth. *Yaksha!*

And Benz was facing him, alone!

—m—

Jennifer's waking up, Benz realized, her ears perking up at movement from inside the car under Yaksha's curled feet. *Glad to see she's alive.*

But it wouldn't mean much if she couldn't get her away from Yaksha!

So what was she going to do? She had her gun, but if he could travel between dimensions without a problem, there was no way bullets could hurt him!

Then again—Benz raised her pistol, took aim, and fired two shots—*why not be sure?* Her bullets hit Yaksha right in one of his black eyes …

And bounced off, harmlessly.

Nuts.

"Let it be known, Julie Benz, that you never turned away when it came to the well-being of your fellow man." Yaksha stood to his full height atop the downed rental car. "It's the reason you're worthy of the lightning and the boons it gave you."

Boons? "What are you—" was all Benz could say before a claw shot out, catching her in the side of the head.

—m—

Benz! Jennifer froze as the detective landed on the ground with a dull thump. *I'm alone!* She felt the car shake around her. Looking frantically for the source, she saw it was coming from above.

It was the sound of metal being ripped apart by bare hands!

Yaksha! Jennifer used her good arm to search for a weapon, her fingers closing around something cylindrical when a white claw punched through the metal above her, leaving a small hole in its place.

Ebony eyes looked at her, razor-sharp teeth flashing in the moonlight.

Jennifer raised her weapon, saw it was ... *A screwdriver? What am I supposed to do with this?!*

Two clawed hands widened the hole just enough for a small body to fit through.

Or for one to be pulled out.

Oh my god! Jennifer gagged as Yaksha's claws reached in, wrapping around her neck. Then, in one swift motion, they yanked her out of the car, and she found herself face-to-face with him.

"Nice to meet you," Yaksha said, giving her an amused look.

Oh my god, where do I look?! Jennifer wondered, not wanting to see one hint of Yaksha's batlike face. "Where's my daughter?!" she rasped as Yaksha casually leapt from the car's roof, landing a few feet away, with her in his iron-grip.

"You've caused much trouble over the past few days," Yaksha declared, giving Jennifer a shrewd look. "Harassing the GCPD about your daughter, bringing attention to their case on the Solomons, keeping people riled up. You've made my job quite challenging."

"You people took my daughter," she rasped, her hands trying to pry his talons from around her throat.

"We punished a killer."

"You took an innocent person!" Jennifer thrashed in Yaksha's grip.

"The child she *murdered* was innocent," the bat-man stated with grim emphasis.

I know that, Jennifer thought angrily. "She's still my daughter!"

"That doesn't give her a free pass."

Stop being so damn calm! "Lots of people have done what she did! Why go after my little girl?!"

"What makes you thinks we're only going after her?" Yaksha asked, holding Jennifer's face a few inches from his own. "Why do you think we let the Solomons work in Gateway City?"

I don't care about this, damn you! I just want Kate back! Jennifer knew she was being selfish, but she didn't care …

Not when the prosecutor recounted the events of Brian Solomon's death at Kate's trial.

Not when Kate's police chief talked to her behind closed doors.

Not even when her husband told her, begged her, to let it go.

It didn't matter—it would never matter. Kate was her child, and she was her mother, and a mother's job is to protect her child.

No matter what.

Yaksha smiled, as though he had heard her thoughts. "You mothers think way too highly of yourselves." He tossed her aside as if she were garbage. "If we let you have your way, there would be no accountability for anyone."

"There'd be understanding," Jennifer coughed as she hit the ground. "There'd be love."

"Tell me, what of Stan and Francine's love for their child? Does it not count? What of your 'love' for them? What of your understanding of their pain?"

"I know it doesn't make sense," Jennifer rasped, slowly getting to her feet despite every iota of her body screaming in pain. "I know it makes me selfish, but that's what being a parent is! Loving your child above all else! That's all that matters!"

"Says a woman who blinds herself to the pain of two hurting parents," Yaksha scoffed, pointing a claw directly at her head. "This conversation is pointless. Time to clean up this mess."

This is it, Jennifer thought, breathing hard while gripping the screwdriver in her good hand. *All this … after everything, to have it end here …* "All right, you son of a bitch! Freaking end me, already!"

"Hey, Mrs. Drama!" a snarky voice called out from the entrance to forest clearing. "Save a little something for the rest of us, eh?!"

Jennifer barely had time to turn her head to the speaker before a gunshot rang out, a bullet catching Yaksha in the side of the head.

—⚊—

"Randal," Yaksha growled, turning to see Stan's father in the center of a hole in the tree line made by Benz and Jennifer's car careening off the road. "What are you doing here?"

Randal Solomon stood there, dressed in jeans and a flannel shirt. He held a shotgun in his hands, aimed right at Yaksha's head. "Something really stupid, but that's life, eh?" He let off another shot, hitting Yaksha's left eye.

He reeled back, letting Jennifer go.

"Randal ...," Jennifer whispered as she fell to the ground.

Randal ran just fast enough to catch her. She looked up, giving him a grateful smile, while blood dripped from both sides of her mouth.

"You're ... pretty fast ... for an old man."

"Easy," Randal said, quickly checking her injuries. "We don't get you to a hospital, you're gonna die."

"Not leaving ... now."

"Getting your daughter back's not gonna matter if you're not alive to see her."

"Wait." Jennifer lifted her head to see Benz's body. "Have to ... help ..."

"Don't worry," Randal said, letting her lean on him as he got to his feet. "They're not gonna kill her. They *need* her."

Who? "Yaksha's masters?"

"No," Randal answered, giving Jennifer a wry smile. "My kids."

"How could you ... possibly know that?"

"You think it was chance that Benz was untouched by a lightning bolt that blew up your daughter's house while she was inside?"

"You tell her too much, old man," Yaksha declared, holding Randal's smoking bullet in his hand as he stood in the center of the forest clearing.

"Old man? Now you done gone and hurt my feelings."

"Randal," Jennifer whispered, fighting to stay conscious. "Can you ... fight him?"

"Not even a little," he answered.

"Then *why* are you ... antagonizing him?!"

"Would you rather I let *you* do it?"

Smartass. "Carry on, then," Jennifer rasped, trying to get her voice back.

177

—〰—

Randal and Jennifer stared at Yaksha.

He stared back, like a coiled snake ready to strike.

Got us dead to rights, Jennifer thought once she could hold a thought in her addled head. *Why isn't he attacking us?* She glanced at her stomach, seeing that the cuts had stopped bleeding. That meant either there was no more blood left in her body or they were healing.

She tried to move her bad arm, only to be rewarded with knives of pain shooting up her shoulder. *Nope! Still not working!*

"Dammit … Randal … what are you waiting for?" Jennifer asked hoarsely, keeping a wary eye on Yaksha. "What are either of you … waiting for?"

Randal's grim smile widened as an explosion rocked the nighttime sky. "Him."

Curious, Jennifer looked up, thinking the sound to be thunder. Then she saw that the sky was clear, the moon hanging above them like a giant silver dollar. *Where'd … thunder come from?*

It hit her as her eyes caught the faint outline of something shooting out of the moon toward them. *Sonic … boom.* And only two people could create that. *Does that mean …*

Someone dropped like a stone between her, Randal, and Yaksha. He kept his back to them, but Jennifer recognized one of her daughter's kidnappers as if he were the back of her hand. *Stan freaking Solomon!*

—〰—

"Yaksha," a baritone voice rang out, so powerful it nearly shook every tree in the clearing. "What's the meaning of this?"

"I could ask you the same question," Yaksha answered in a calm voice.

They know each other! Jennifer's mind sputtered in disbelief. *They freaking know … each other!* Randal told them as much, but to see living proof of it, right before her eyes!

The one good one, anyway.

"Why are you threatening my father?" Stan demanded hotly. "That's in direct violation of our agreement!"

"Your father is interfering in my operation," Yaksha answered as he folded his wings around his shoulders. It gave the illusion of him wearing a cape. "*That* is also a violation of our agreement!"

"Dad"—Stan looked over his shoulder, his eyes blazing fire—"is that true?"

"How about you watch your tone and turn off those eye beams?!" Randal snapped back.

Stan's anger grew as his gaze landed on Jennifer. "How about I leave you and her to Yaksha, with my blessing?"

Randal was taken aback. "You ungrateful—"

"Dad," Stan blurted out, his voice firm, "is Yaksha telling the truth?!"

Yaksha stood there, his ivory-colored form looking like a teacher waiting to hear a confession from an unruly student who had just been caught.

"Yes," Randal hissed, "dammit."

"Wow. Just freaking wow." Stan shook his head in disapproval before turning to face the bat-man. "I apologize, Yaksha. I thought *you* were the aggressor."

"An honest mistake," Yaksha said, grinning in understanding. "One I admittedly played a part in."

—⟨⟨⟩⟩—

"How can you talk to him so casually ... after what he's done?!" Jennifer rasped despite her weakened state. "How?!"

Stan turned to the car, his eyes widening in shock at seeing Benz's prone body. "Oh God, Yaksha ..."

"She's unhurt," the pale bat-man said as Stan bolted to the fallen detective.

"I see cuts and bruises all over her body!"

"Okay. Moderately unhurt," Yaksha corrected after giving the fallen detective a quick glance, "but she got in the way of my operation too."

"Oh yeah!" Randal shouted sarcastically. "Run to help the detective! Don't worry about your dear old dad!"

Stan cradled Benz in his arms, calling her name gently.

If Jennifer didn't know any better, she would think they were lovers. *How'd Stan's arrival … change things so quickly?*

And why'd he care about Detective Benz so much?

Wait a minute … Jennifer thought back to Randal's earlier comment about how the Solomons needed her for something. *She's not in cahoots with them, is she?*

—⚬—

Benz's eyes fluttered open, and the first thing she saw was Stan's face. "Wondered when we'd meet again."

"We keep meeting like this, people are gonna talk," he declared, carefully helping her up to a sitting position.

Real cute. Benz saw Yaksha standing across from her and reached for her gun, only to see it lying across the clearing. *Crap, how'd* that *happen?*

"Everyone, relax," Stan said, getting Benz to her feet. "There's been enough craziness here."

"You're one to talk!" Jennifer Barrow bellowed from where she stood with … Randal Solomon? "You kidnapped my little girl!"

"Your 'little girl' committed an adult crime." Stan turned his full gaze on her. "And got an adult punishment."

"She was acquitted, damn you!"

"By a racist kangaroo court. But not by me, or my wife."

"Just because the justice system didn't grovel at your feet doesn't make it racist!"

—⚬—

"Nice one," Randal whispered icily in her ear. "What are you gonna say next? That racism doesn't exist? We *love* hearing that one!"

"Then what do *you* suggest I say?!" Jennifer demanded as she blinked a drop of sweat from her eye. *God, my body hurts!*

"Try talking to him like a parent who lost a child, not a servant that has to do what you want!"

"I am *not* going to grovel to him!"

"You want your daughter back or not?!"

"You think I haven't sacrifice anything?!" Jennifer looked from Randal to Stan, feeling as though there was some cosmic joke everyone was in on except her. "Officer Jacobson?! My marriage?! My reputation?! Haven't I sacrificed enough?!"

"Oh, boo-hoo," Randal spat in a bitter voice. "Stan's got the power here! Not you!"

"Stop saying that!"

"It took a lot for me to get Stan here," Randal added, his body feeling tense against hers. "Make it count, woman!"

Goddammit, he's right. Jennifer looked to Stan, who was still holding Benz. *He is being gentle with her. Means he can be talked to. Reasoned with.* "I guess ..."

"Trust me, you *don't* want Francine here."

Got my whole life to be angry. Only got right now to get Kate back! "Stan, wait!" Jennifer shouted, feeling another piece of her self-respect fall away. "I'm sorry about what I said! I have to talk to you!"

—⚅—

NOW she's easy to work with, Benz thought, rolling her eyes with disdain. *Unbelievable!*

"And now she wants to hear what I have to say," Stan muttered, giving Jennifer an uneasy glance. "Now that I got something she wants."

"You mean *someone*." Benz gingerly felt the side of her head where Yaksha hit her. Her hand came away with surprisingly little blood. "Her daughter."

"What is my father doing here?" Stan asked, shrugging off Benz's comment.

"We sought him out," she said, hoping to keep Randal out of his crosshairs. "Mrs. Barrow found his address, came here to confront him. I came with her."

"Why are you here helping her?"

"I want to bring Kate home, just as she does." *Maybe even more so.*

"Funny how you and the damn police department are bending over backwards to help the mother of my son's killer, but wouldn't lift a finger

181

to help me or my wife," Stan spat out hatefully. "Being a white mother must be great!"

"Don't say that," Benz beseeched him quietly. "She had to give up a lot to be here."

Stan's deep voice rumbled with exasperation as he scoffed. "Not nearly as much as me and my wife, Detective. Not *nearly* as much."

—⚬⚬—

"So," Yaksha said as he approached Jennifer and Randal. "What to do about you ..."

"Don't come near us." Jennifer tried to step back, but Randal wouldn't budge. "We'll fight you if we have to!"

Yaksha let out a laugh that sounded like a drowning cat. "Good luck with that!"

"Lady," Randal said, shaking his head, "don't give him any ideas."

"What? I'm defending us!"

"It wouldn't be me he'd hurt."

What are you ... Then she saw it in his eyes, the stark realization of her place in the scheme of things. The way Yaksha was going to kill her, until Randal arrived. How he then stayed his hand until Stan came on the scene.

The talk between him and Yaksha about having an "agreement" ...

Not to mention how Randal talked about him getting Yaksha and Stan to meet ...

Randal's protected, Jennifer realized as her eyes flicked from him, to Yaksha, to Stan. *That's why he arrived when he did. Dammit, that's why he was so quick to get us out of his home. He knew Yaksha was watching Benz and me.*

Jennifer's eyes widened ever so slightly, her pupils dilating with the realization that had suddenly become apparent. She slowly wet her lips, the tip of her tongue darting out to brush against them. *Our being in his home was putting his neighbors in danger ... FROM us!*

But what about Benz?

No. Jennifer saw again how tender Stan was with her. *She's protected too.*

That just leaves me. The realization left her weak in the knees. *I'm the one with a target on her back.* She glanced first at Randal, then at Yaksha. He turned away while Yaksha stared back at her, confirming what she had just realized.

I'm not going to get a fair shake in this no matter what I do. Jennifer recalled Randal's words about racism. They were the same words that the press and people on the street had said during Kate's trial. A fresh new fear washed over her, settling in her stomach like a stone. *Just like the Solomons at Kate's trial.*

—◊—

"How about that?" Stan watched Jennifer from where he stood, looking impressed. "She gets it. I should kidnap people more often."

But Benz didn't find it funny. As far as she was concerned, no one should fear being singled out for being who they are. "Mr. Solomon, you made your point."

Stan turned to face her. "Excuse me?"

"Look at her, Mr. Solomon. If you wanted her to feel the way you felt when the courts acquitted Kate of your son's death, mission accomplished."

"It's not enough."

That didn't mean they weren't true.

"And what do you suggest, eh? Justice? We tried that." Stan's eyes narrowed into slits. "It failed us."

"Not justice, Mr. Solomon," Benz answered, matching his hard expression with her own. "Mercy."

—◊—

"Seeing it now?" Yaksha asked as though he could read Jennifer's thoughts.

"Yeah," she answered bitterly. "I do. But that's not gonna stop me from trying to save my little girl."

"She's not a baby," Yaksha declared, glowering at Jennifer. "She's a grown woman, who committed a grownup crime."

"Stop saying that!" Jennifer snapped; her hands balled into shaking fists even as her angry words made her head hurt. "Our children will always be our babies no matter how much people try to tell us differently! It's the same for me, for him," Jennifer tilted her head toward Randal, who thankfully nodded in agreement, "and the same for ..."

Yaksha nodded his head, as if waiting for her to say it. "Go on."

"The Solomons." *Dammit.* Jennifer winced, as though she had been slapped. *I walked into that.*

Brian Solomon had been Stan and Francine's baby, too.

And Jennifer's baby, Kate, took him away from them. And unlike her, they would never get him back. Jennifer could cry and complain all she wanted about her rights as a parent, but if human law wouldn't respect the Solomons' rights as parents, why would Yaksha's law respect hers?

—⟋⟍⟍—

Stan arched his brow in surprise, clearly not expecting Benz's answer.

Got you, didn't I? "The beings that gave you and your wife powers, they heard your story," Benz continued in a knowing voice. "They showed you understanding. All I'm asking you to do is show Mrs. Barrow the same."

"Detective—"

"The same mercy you showed me the night you and Francine took Kate ..."

Stan kept trying to get a word in. "Don't misunderstand—"

"When you shielded me from the lightning bolt Francine called from the sky, right when it demolished Kate's home."

Stan squared his shoulders, his gaze trained on her. After a few minutes, he let out a defeated smile. "You caught that, huh?"

"I've seen enough superhero movies to know superspeed when I see it," Benz answered, giving him a conspiratorial wink. "How else did I survive Francine's bolt unscathed while it destroyed a house we were *inside* of?"

Stan chuckled without mirth, shaking his head. "Francine told me you'd figure that out."

Smart lady. Not the calmest, though. "All I'm asking you to do is show that same mercy to Mrs. Barrow. Just hear her out. That's all you have to do."

"You just want to do that because you think I'll help her, no questions asked."

"No," Benz said, shaking her head. "I don't know what you'll do. I'm not arrogant enough to think I do. All I want you to do is listen to her story. What you decide is up to you." *Please, Stan! She won't stop otherwise!*

"Fine," he agreed. "But I make no promises. And the *second* I don't like what she says, I'm gone."

Yes! Yes! Yes! Benz fought the urge to pump her fists in triumph. "I'll take what I can get." She gingerly put her weight on his shoulder. "So, shall we?"

"Fine." Using one arm to support her weight, Stan floated over to Yaksha, Randal, and Jennifer.

—⚂—

He's coming, Jennifer thought, seeing Stan Solomon approaching. *He's coming!* Maybe it was the blood loss making her loopy, but she was struck by how handsome he was.

Dressed in a dark-blue bodysuit with a long cape flowing behind him, he really did look like a superhero. A demented one, but a superhero, to be sure.

And those eyes. Brown as milk chocolate, they seemed to glow with an inviting light all their own.

This man took your daughter. Jennifer's cheeks burned with shame at having to be reminded of such a thing. *For doing her job.*

No, for killing his son.

"I believe you have something you want to tell me," Stan said after giving her an exacting look.

"Yes," Jennifer said, swallowing back a wave of uneasiness. *Those eyes ...* "You have my daughter."

"No. The Other Side has your daughter."

185

My daughter's prison has a trendy name. Freaking wonderful. "I want you to—I need you to bring her back." Jennifer cleared her throat, which had gone dry all of a sudden.

"And I want my son to still be alive," Stan stated in a heavy, grief-stricken voice laden with anger. "Tell me, will bringing his killer back make that happen?"

You know it won't. Jennifer didn't want to say it, but she didn't know what else to say. "No," she said finally, shaking her head. "It won't."

"Your haggling skills are amazing," Randal sad in a snarky voice, keeping his eyes on Stan's chest. He didn't even look at his son's eyes.

Did he feel the same sense of failure that Jennifer did?

The same guilt, perhaps, that Benz felt?

We go through all the trouble of bringing you two together, and of course, you don't know what to say. Benz rolled her eyes in annoyance at Jennifer's hesitation. *I gotta do everything!*

"I have absolutely no reason to help you," Stan said, shaking his head with a grim smile. "Turn around and go home, before I let my partner have his way with you." He tilted his head toward Yaksha.

Yaksha, in return, gave the rest of them a salute.

Pretty regimented for a monster. Benz gazed at Yaksha with barely concealed curiosity. *What's the real nature of their relationship?*

"Son," Randal spoke up, looking Stan in the eye. "Just hear her out …"

"How can you be with her?" Stan blew up, his eyes wild with rage. "Helping her? Her?! After what her kin did to our family!"

"I know what her kin took from us!" Randal snapped back. "But keeping her as a prisoner's not gonna bring Brian back!"

"Neither will bringing her back like nothing happened!"

"Her name is Kate," Jennifer cut in weakly. "Kate Barrow. Kate Josephine Barrow, and she's my daughter." She calmed down as the two men stopped their fighting to look at her.

Correction, Randal looked at her. Stan glared at her.

You got their attention, Benz thought, looking at men that represented two generations of an embattled and scarred family. *Now make it count. Say the right thing!* She desperately wanted this—the Solomons, Kate's kidnapping, and the resentment it created—to end.

More than anything, Benz wanted her part in it to end. She wanted to go back to being a regular, no-name cop. She was tired of being a witness to the arrival of the Solomons.

"She's twenty-five years old," Jennifer continued, emboldened by the attention her words held. "She's loves horses and '80s synth music. She volunteers in soup kitchens for the homeless every year during Christmas. When she was in college, she worked with Habitat For Humanity to build homes for the needy. She was in Greenpeace, for cripes sake!"

"Congratulations, she was a good person," Stan said dismissively. "Doing what everyone should be doing."

"You did the same when you were her age," Randal cut in. "She wanted to help people, son. Just like you did. Just like me and your mother raised you to do."

"Too bad she didn't bother to help our son."

C'mon, Stan! Benz gawked helplessly at his grim expression. *Show me the good I saw when you and Francine took Kate! I know it's there!*

As if sensing that he wanted to do more than just stand around, Randal lifted Jennifer off the ground, hoisting her up until she was about eye level with Stan. Jennifer then reached out, placing a bloodied hand on Stan's shoulder.

He swatted it away, glaring at her.

"If Kate could've sacrificed herself to bring Brian back," Jennifer declared, refusing to back down, "she would have."

Yes! Jennifer rejoiced inside as Stan, his father, and Benz did a collective double take. *I got through!* "I know Kate couldn't begin to know what you and your wife were going through at the loss of your son. No one really can, unless they're a parent. But she knew guilt. And was buried by it."

"Was she?" Stan asked sarcastically. "Was she *really*?"

"Yes. She didn't show it during the trial because she was told not to, by her legal team and the GCPD—something I did *not* endorse," Jennifer explained in a raspy voice. "But when it was just Kate and me, I saw the guilt eating her up inside. I felt it. We all did."

"Brian died drowning in his own blood," Stan stated coldly. "Did you know that?"

"Jesus, son," Randal swore, holding his stomach. "I had dinner before coming out here!"

"Don't you *even* say I'm going too far!" Stan glared at him, while stabbing a finger at Jennifer's face. "Not after all *her* kid's done!"

"Did you know she visited Brian's grave after he was buried?"

"Dammit, Mrs. Barrow ..."

"She did," Jennifer continued as she barely clung to consciousness. *Losing so much blood!* "Every day. Her chief put her on leave because she couldn't do her job after Brian was killed. And she tried too. But she couldn't. You want to know why?"

"Let me guess," Stan answered sarcastically. "Because she saw him everywhere! I'm sure to her we *all* look alike!"

Stop twisting my words! For everything Jennifer said, Stan had a ready response. Even for things she hadn't said yet! Almost as if ... A lightbulb went off in her head. "You spoke to Kate!"

"Did you think we wouldn't?" Stan demanded. "When Francine and I arrived at her home, which was *way* too nice for someone on a cop's salary, she told us all of this!"

—⚹—

That's right, Benz thought. *When we arrived at her house, the Solomons already had Kate tied up. They worked her over. Kate must've told them something—anything—to make the pain stop. I just didn't know how much she told them.*

"Francine didn't want to just take her," Stan continued, coming very close to ranting. "That would've been too simple! No, she wanted Kate to recount how she killed our son, in excruciating detail!"

"Crap, that sounds like something Frannie would do," Randal muttered under his breath. "Just to dig the knife in deeper."

And to make Kate face what she did, Benz thought woefully. Francine had been a teacher before Brian's death. And like a teacher, she wouldn't be satisfied with a simple answer to a problem.

She'd want to see the work.

"That …" Jennifer looked as though she had been sucker-punched. "Reliving that horror … must've broke Kate …"

"It sure as hell broke us," Stan stated, nodding his head slowly. "But it also told us the truth."

"Which is?"

"That 'Kate' didn't *see* our son. All she saw was this"—Stan stabbed a finger at the black skin of his exposed hand— "and opened fire. Just like the rest of the GCPD and police officers all over the country. That's all they see, and that's the only excuse they need."

"Making some *pretty* big generalizations, Stan," Benz recoiled, Stan words feeling like bullets to her. She had told Frank the same things during their time in their squad car, but never so rough. "You know all of us aren't like that."

"Of course I do, but guess what? The rest of you aren't doing enough to stop the ones that are. And all the protesting, and marching, and lobbying in the world is not going to change that. Not as long as bloodthirsty cops think they can get away with murder. As long as the law lets them do that, they will."

"So that's what you think this is?" Benz could finally see the train Stan was on. "You making a stand?"

"I'm sending a message," Stan corrected her, turning to face her. "Kate Barrow needed to be made an example. To let her fellow joy-boys know that their behavior would no longer be tolerated!"

Jesus, Benz thought, an aghast look on her face. It was a look Randal and Jennifer shared. *Do you know what you sound like?*

"She needed to be punished," Stan stated with a chilling finality. "And she was. For being a racist. For being incompetent. And for not being better than those that came before her."

—◊◊◊—

189

The wind blew through the trees, bringing bitter chill with it. It matched the sense of hopelessness that threatened to swallow Jennifer whole.

This is why I didn't want you to be a cop, Kate, she thought, seeing fully what her daughter's actions had created. *Because you'd be holding people's lives in your hands. And when you mess up, you create monsters.*

And in Stan Solomon and his wife, Kate had created two.

Monsters, fueled by a justifiable anger that drove every action they took and every word they spoke. Stan kept his in check, but it was there. Burning like a fire behind his eyes.

Francine Solomon, from what little Jennifer had learned from Benz, was worse. A towering inferno of rage, compared to Stan's small campfire.

A mother's rage, born from an innate desire to annihilate anyone that threatened her child.

Just like Jennifer was doing for Kate. Except she couldn't attack Stan or Francine. She needed them to get Kate back!

Searching for the right words, Jennifer looked up at the sky. Saw to her surprise that the moon still hung above them. In fact … *It hasn't moved since Stan arrived.*

Jennifer looked back at him, a puzzled look on her face. *Is he … holding it in place?* She looked over his shoulder to Yaksha. *Or is he? How would either of them be doing that?*

Or maybe they weren't. Maybe they were somehow freezing the moment, like in one of those science fiction shows Kate watched when she was a kid. *Shit, Kate! Think about Kate!*

She turned back to Stan, a crazy, unthinkable plan forming in her mind. "What do I have to do to get Kate back?"

He took a step back, a wary expression on his face. "Excuse me?"

"You heard me," Jennifer said, angry that Stan chose right then to be deaf. "What do I have to do to get Kate back?"

"Are you trying to make a deal with me?"

"Jennifer," Randal cautioned, "that's not a good idea."

"You told me I'd have to give up something to get my daughter back," she hissed under her breath. "Pleading's not working, and neither's relating to him, so bargaining's all I have left!" She had no idea what Stan wanted—besides Brian up and around again—but she'd do everything in her power to give it to him.

Anything to get Kate back.

—⚊—

Oh Jennifer, Benz thought, her heart in her throat. *What are you doing?*

"What do you think you can do?" Stan asked in a flippant voice. "Give us another son?"

"If I have to," Jennifer answered, not batting an eye.

"I …" Stan's mouth hung agape in shock. "You're sick."

"I'm desperate, dammit!" Jennifer blurted out, the words dripping with feral frustration. She tumbled from Randal's grip, her head hanging on drooping shoulders. "You think I want to do this?!" She caught herself before hitting the ground. "I don't, damn you! But I'll do anything to get Kate back! I've tried begging you! I've reasoned with you, and God help me, I even tried empathizing with you! Nothing has worked! So I'm trying this!"

My God, she's serious, Benz thought, giving her a look that jumped between shock and disgust. *She just … propositioned Stan Solomon, in front of all of us!* She looked to Stan, saw that he looked as stunned— and disgusted—and she did. *How the hell would she even … Could she even …*

Could Jennifer even bring a child from Stan to term? And how would she even give birth, given her age?

That, and that fact that she was human while Stan no longer was?

Shooting his son a disgusted look, Randal led Jennifer away from Stan, Benz, and Yaksha to sit on a nearby rock. Harsh rasping sounds came from her lips as she put her full weight on the rock. Despite that, her rummy eyes kept their gaze on Stan, as if awaiting an answer.

She's delirious, Benz thought, seeing for the first time the full extent of her injuries. The bleeding from the cuts and scrapes on her body had subsided, but the blood loss had clearly affected Jennifer's mind. Why else would she proposition Stan the way she did? *I hope I never get that desperate.*

"Stan," Randal bellowed, stomping back to get in his son's face. "Is this what you want?! To get a mom turning tricks? Is this what Brian would want?!"

"You don't get to tell me what my son wants!" Stan let go of Benz, taking a deadly step toward the older man. "You weren't there for him! You didn't even raise him! And you can't bully me into doing what you want!"

"The only bully here is you, son," Randal declared, stabbing a finger at his face.

"You don't get to call me that," Stan thundered back, his eyes wide with anger.

"Stop!" Benz stepped between the two men. "This is getting us nowhere!" She glanced over her shoulder, seeing Jennifer trying to stay conscious. *This was a mistake. Meeting Randal. Bringing Jennifer along. Especially coming without backup, it's all been one big mistake!*

"So you think you're the big shit now, huh?!" Randal took another step toward Stan. "Then prove it, Mr. Big Man! Prove you're more than the man who couldn't even protect his own son!"

No, no, no! Benz felt Stan's dry heat wash over her. His eyes grew wide as lightning crackled in the sky. Thunder rocked the clearing, drowning out her cry as Stan drew his hand back ...

And let fly a massive backhand that sent Randal flying across the forest clearing!

—⚋—

Randal hit the ground with a solid *oomph!* The grass cushioned the impact, but it didn't make the sight of him skittering across it any easier to watch.

"Stan, what have you done?!" Benz ran to him, her injuries forgotten as she knelt by Randal's side. "Mr. Solomon! Are you okay?!"

To her surprise, he sat up immediately. Glaring at Stan, he spat out a wad of blood. "All that power, and you *still* hit like a weak-ass bitch."

—⚋—

What did he just say?! Jennifer wondered, looking on, perplexed.

Benz recoiled, taking a step back from Randal as he got to his feet.

"And you're still a misogynist," Stan spat as he stood his ground. "Francine couldn't undo that. But she keeps trying, even making you immune to our powers!"

He's one of them. Jennifer's breath caught in her throat. *Is Benz one of them too?*

"Frannie respects her father," Randal declared as he took a threatening step toward him. "A lesson I'm gonna beat into you right now!"

"Randal! Stop!" Jennifer shouted hoarsely. "This isn't helping me get Kate back!"

"This isn't helping anything," Benz declared, stepping boldly between two generations of raging Solomons. She held out her hands, touching the chest of each man. "I do not want to fight the two of you—"

Fight them? Jennifer looked at her as if she were crazy. *What can she do?!*

"As much as I'm sure that would be entertaining to Mrs. Barrow here," Yaksha cut in, sounding way too logical, given what he looked like. "I believe I have a solution that will satisfy all parties."

As much as she didn't want to listen to anyone that looked like an ivory-colored demon, Jennifer turned her gaze to him. She noticed everyone else did too.

"Stan, it is clear that you did not want to take Kate Barrow in the first place," Yaksha declared, stepping into the middle of the clearing. "And I can tell from your body language that you feel guilty for keeping her from her family."

"I do," he agreed. "But taking her sent a message. I bring her back, that message will be undone."

There's that phrase again! "What message could taking my little girl possibly—" Jennifer choked off her words as Yaksha raised a cautionary claw and then pointed it at her. "You don't need to hold Kate Barrow to send that message."

Stan stared at him, a confused look on his face. "And why is that?"

"I think I know," Benz chimed in.

"Because I also took one of their own," Yaksha answered proudly. "Their very worst, in fact."

—⚏—

The very worst? Benz wondered, confusion on her face. *Who could he be talking about?* Then it hit her, like a lightning bolt to the brain. "You're talking about Jacobson."

"The very same," Yaksha said, bowing slightly to her.

"Oh, I remember him," Stan growled angrily. "I broke his arm when he tried to manhandle my Francine after Kate killed Brian!"

Of course you remember that, Benz thought warily. *For cripes' sake, do you have any good memories of us?* "Is he still alive?"

"We," Yaksha said pointedly, "aren't here to talk about him. We're here to talk about Kate Barrow." He turned to Stan. "We have Jacobson. And if the detective is here, her people *know* we have him."

Now hold on a minute! "The GCPD has no idea I'm here!"

"Your people don't do anything without telling someone higher in the food chain. Like, perhaps, an Inspector Isenguard?"

Has he been following me? Benz froze where she stood. "How'd you—?" Yaksha smiled, his eyes shining with triumphant superiority. "When I brought Jacobson before my superiors, he revealed a *great* many things."

I do not *like the sound of those words.* "Why'd you even take him?!"

"One, he got in the way of my cleanup operation," Yaksha began, raising another claw, "repeatedly." He raised a third one. "Two, he has a history of police brutality and witness intimidation going back years. He told us as much."

"That can't be true."

"Jacobson told us your police chief knew of this and did nothing but sweep it under the rug. For years."

"Who's 'us'?" Benz demanded, using air quotes while glancing at Yaksha's scaly chest. In the middle of it, she saw a symbol. It was like the symbol on Stan and Francine's costumes, but smaller. While theirs were the outstretched wings of a bird that took up their chests and shoulders, Yaksha's was a fourth of that size.

It looked like a star in the middle of his chest.

For some reason, it made Benz think of her own detective badge. *Wait a minute …* She looked from the symbol to his face. *He's intelligent. Calculating. Playing the peacemaker while the rest of us are ready to go to war. He talks about having superiors, meaning he reports to a chain of command. And he knew I'd do the same thing before coming here with Jennifer ...*

Benz's jaw dropped as an undeniable realization hit her. *Yaksha's a police officer. Or at the very least his people's equivalent of one.* Which meant everything he had done, not just to Jacobson but to the Barrow family, was on behalf of a higher authority.

Like ... the Arbiters!

—✲—

Losing ... consciousness ... Jennifer's injuries were finally taking their toll. It was a miracle she hadn't passed out sooner, something she attributed to adrenaline. She'd been so pumped to get Kate back; she hadn't had time to feel any pain.

But now that she had finally sat down, her body was taking stock. And judging from the waves of nausea that washed over her, it did not like what it saw. Jennifer threw a hand out, not caring where it went as long as what it touched gave her strength.

Remember ... Kate, Jennifer's mind sputtered as her eyelids grew heavy. *All of this ... for Kate.* Her body got as far as getting her to her knees, before falling back on the rock she sat on. The pitiful whimper she gave off made Randal and Benz glance in her direction.

"Jesus Christ," Randal cursed as he ran to her side. "We gotta get her to a hospital, or she's not gonna make it!"

"Not ... without ...," Jennifer whispered as she melted against his steady frame.

"Kate, I know," he whispered as he cradled her in his arms. "Dammit, I know!" He looked up at Stan and Yaksha. "For God's sake, will you two decide *something*?!"

"Please ...," Jennifer murmured weakly.

—✲—

"Stan, please," Benz said desperately. "Whatever message you wanted to put out by taking Kate Barrow, you got it with Jacobson." *I can't believe I just said that.* "You don't need Kate Barrow anymore! But her family does!"

Stan stood still as a statue, his arms folded over his chest. If not for his gaze bouncing between her and Jennifer, Benz would've sworn he had gone catatonic. "Stan?" *When did I start calling him by his first name?*

Finally, Stan settled his gaze on Jennifer, his jaw clenched.

Benz could only imagine the battle going on inside of him. On the one hand, Yaksha was right. On the other hand, if he let her go, he would face the wrath of a higher authority.

His wife, Francine Solomon.

Happy wife, happy life, as they say, Benz thought, rolling her eyes. *Something* else *to worry about!*

Stan glanced skyward as thunder rumbled, his lips twisted into a sneer. He nodded, as though the thunder itself was talking to him.

Is Francine up there? Benz followed his gaze, her heart hammering in her chest. *Is she listening to our entire conversation?*

God help them if she was!

Stan nodded again, lowering his head to look at Jennifer. His expression was steady, his lips a firm line on his dark face.

Looks like his mind's made up. Benz exchanged looks with Randal. "Stan?"

He looked away from them and shot into the nighttime sky, loud as a gunshot.

Dammit, Benz cursed, watching Stan's ascent. *So much for that.* "Okay, Yaksha, I got some questions for—"

To her chagrin, the bat-man-looking alien was gone. *Dammit!*

"Guess we got our answer," Randal stated sadly. "From both of 'em."

"Yeah, we did," Benz agreed half-heartedly. *No matter how much I don't like it.* She looked to Jennifer. "Let's get you patched—"

She had passed out in Randal's arms.

—∞—

Jennifer's eyes fluttered open to see the inside of a hospital room. "How'd I …" She let out a savage cough that awoke someone sitting at her bedside.

"Good to see you're awake," Randal said cordially as he scooted his chair closer. "Had us worried for a minute."

My throat hurts! Jennifer gingerly massaged her neck. "Could I have a …"

A glass of water seemingly materialized in Randal's hand, which he handed to her. "Don't move too quick, princess. You'll pull your stitches."

"What … hospital is this?"

"Duke Hospital," Randal answered, flashing a proud smile. "Not too shabby, eh?"

"How … long have I been here?"

"A couple days. After you passed out, this was the best place to take you."

Jennifer raised her left hand, her right one in a cast. In her good arm was an IV attached to monitors next to her bedside. "How bad was I hurt?"

"Main damage were the cuts in your stomach." Randal walked to a fountain to get her another cup of water. "The surgeons stitched them up, but you won't be wearing any two-piece bathing suits for a while."

Right, that's *my main concern.* "Where's Benz?"

"Talking to our police department. She's in some hot water for working a case in their jurisdiction without so much as a hello," Randal answered grimly, returning to her bedside with her second cup of water. "I'm gonna raise you into a sitting position." Randal pushed a button on a remote he held in his other hand.

Shit! Jennifer bit back a groan of pain as the upper half of her bed lifted her head and torso into an upright position, giving her a better view of her room. *Wait, hold on …* "Am I the only patient in this room?"

"Well, look around," Randal said, gesturing to the room. "Don't you feel special?"

"Did we get Kate back?"

Randal's shoulders sagged. "No."

"Then no." Jennifer looked at the ceiling miserably. "I just feel stupid." She knuckled aching, bloodshot eyes. "Really stupid."

—⋘—

"Jennifer," Benz said as she entered her hospital room. "It is good to see you awake!"

"Thank you," came the humble reply. "I guess I got you and Randal to thank for that. How did you get me here, anyway?"

"Mr. Solomon here had a cell phone. Once Stan and Yaksha left, it started working, and he called 911."

"After all we've been through, Detective? Just call me Randal."

Benz smiled, happy to see him warming up to her. And to Jennifer. She spied the cup of water in her hands, suspected he had gotten it for her. *At least there's something good out of all this.* "Did you know Randal stayed by your bedside every day until you woke up, Jennifer?"

The older woman gave Randal an amused look. "You didn't tell me that."

"A real man …" Randal paused. "A real person doesn't demand credit for doing the right thing. Besides, with what my son's done, it was the least I could do."

Stan. Looking behind her to make sure no one had heard, Benz quietly closed the door, giving the three of them some privacy. "We have to get our stories straight," she said quietly. "A lot of folks outside these doors have a lot of questions and won't be polite much longer to get answers."

"What did you tell them?" Jennifer asked after loudly clearing her throat.

"I steered them to my superiors in Gateway City. My chief told them everything."

"So they know my son was here." Randal let out a weary sigh. "Which means *my* police are gonna be harassing me. Fucking wonderful."

"You and me both." Benz thought of the warning that Inspector Isenguard gave her before leaving Jennifer in her custody. *I took it seriously, and things still went wrong!*

"You gonna get it in the neck?"

Like you wouldn't believe. "Let's just say I'm the problem detective, now."

"I'm sorry, Benz. You too, Randal," Jennifer muttered solemnly. "I'm sorry for *all* of this."

"This isn't your fault, Jennifer," Benz said quickly. "You were just trying to get your daughter back."

"Being a parent doesn't give me a free pass to do whatever I want. It doesn't give me the right to ignore the fact that my daughter is a full-fledged adult that killed an innocent child." Jennifer swallowed quietly. "Or the pain she caused."

"Doesn't give my kids the right to do what they did, either," Randal added, a pained look on his face. "No matter how 'right' it might seem to them."

Looks like we had a meeting of the minds, Benz thought, thoroughly impressed by the about-face the two parents had done. "Are you giving up, Jennifer?"

"I'm just tired, Benz." A solitary tear ran down her cheek. "I have nothing left."

—∿—

Jennifer barely acknowledged Randal as he wheeled her out of Duke Hospital a few days later, with Benz at his side providing police escort. She didn't react as they lifted her into his squad car and belted her in. She sat silent and sullen as they drove to Randal's home.

She didn't even raise her head as Benz put a plate of food in front of her before going off to talk to Randal about … something.

Jennifer was in the process of limping from his bedroom to the kitchen to make a late-night snack, when her stomach scars tingled. *What is …?* Her eyes widened to the size of dinner plates. *Could it be?! Tell me please that it's …*

"Jennifer!" Randal called out from the living room. "Think you better come out here!"

Please! Please! Please! Hurriedly, she hobbled to the living room, not caring how many stitches she ripped. The door that led outside the

199

apartment was open, Randal standing on the other side. He and Benz stared at something in the yard in the back of the complex.

Standing there, with the sky thundering above his head, was Stan Solomon. In his arms was a woman bundled up in a dark sheet. With a hand, he pulled it back, revealing the very alive face of Kate Barrow.

Oh my god! Her injuries forgotten, Jennifer ran just as Stan extended his arms to her. Just when she was a step away from holding her baby girl, he let Kate fall from his arms. She hit the ground hard, a pained groan issuing from her lips.

"Oh, my baby girl!" Jennifer wept as she fiercely cradled a child she feared she would never see again.

"M-Mom?" Kate stammered, sounding much younger than her twenty-five years. Her blond hair was wet and matted against her face, her eyes vacant and unseeing. She shivered, as if in the grip of hypothermia.

"Thank you." Jennifer looked up, Stan a dark blur through tears of joy. "Thank you! Thank you! Thank you!"

"You owe me now, Mrs. Barrow," came the cold reply. "You've a debt to my family. One you will pay at the time of our choosing. Without argument."

Before she could say anything, Stan floated past her.

—◆◆◆—

I've seen this before, Benz thought as Stan approached her and Randal. Her hand hovered near her sidearm, knowing it was just a symbolic gesture. Her other hand inched to her cell phone in her pocket, but a grim look from Stan told her that was a bad idea.

"Let me guess. You feel all mad and wanna take it out on me, huh?!" Randal raised his fists. "C'mon, then!"

"Randal! Shut! Up!" Benz hissed through clenched teeth. "Enough of this machismo crap! It's not helping anything!"

"You are the smart one." Stan's lips lifted up into a smirk. "You actually care."

"I care for all people," Benz declared passionately. "I know you do too."

"I still do." Stan turned his head to Randal. "When they deserve it."

"For God's sake, Stan! He was only trying to help us!"

"You stood with the mother of my son's killer," Stan stated, his eyes locked on his father. "The detective, I understand. But you? You betrayed my family."

"I'd do it again," Randal declared. "Anything to make this cycle of misery stop."

"You did it for her," Stan cocked his head in Jennifer's direction. "So we are done."

"Wait." Randal's brow arched, a look of concern on his face. "What do you mean, done?"

"Any protection you had from us has been rescinded," Stan answered in a voice as grim and pitiless as the Grim Reaper's. "Do not come to Gateway City. If you do, you will die."

Randal looked speechless, his lips trying to form proper words.

"Also, tell Kate to not scratch at the wall."

"What does that mean?" Benz asked. "Stan! What does that mean?!" Before either she or Randal could say anything else, he shot up into the sky, taking the thunder with him.

—◆—

Jennifer rocked Kate in her arms, radiating a profound sense of accomplishment.

Then she noticed how cold Kate was.

Concerned, she looked into her daughter's eyes …

And felt as though she was falling into a nest of spiders.

It was only a second, but it made Jennifer shudder. It was as though she realized that while she meant to do the right thing, she, in fact, had done wrong.

But the second passed, and she sang to Kate as though she were a child again.

To Be Continued…

www.ingramcontent.com/pod-product-compliance
Lightning Source LLC
Chambersburg PA
CBHW020842260626
47169CB00003B/1103